Infidelity for Beginners

Danny King

Infidelity for Beginners

Copyright © 2020 Danny King

ALL RIGHTS RESERVED

No part of this book may be reproduced in any form, by photocopying or by any electronic or mechanical means, including information storage or retrieval systems, without permission in writing from the copyright owner.

All characters and events in this book are fictitious. Any similarity to real persons, living or dead, is coincidental and not intended by the author.

Cover art by the author

Third edition

First published in 2013 by Byker Books.

ISBN: 979-855042541-1

AUTHOR NOTE

This edition of *Infidelity for Beginners* was released by the author. It was first published in paperback in 2013 by Byker Books and is republished now with the kind permission of Andy Rivers. Do check out Andy's own books at www.bykerbooks.co.uk because he is, in this own words, *Radge* (it's a Geordie term, apparently).

Danny

For Andrew Crockett
a tireless champion of my books and the best gosh-darn
brother-in-law any skint writer could wish for.

You may find yourself in a beautiful house, with a beautiful wife. You may ask yourself, "Well, how did I get here?"

– 'Once in a Lifetime', Talking Heads

CHAPTER 1.
WE'RE NOT EXACTLY CURING CANCER HERE

"… SO YOU SEE we're having to check overheads in every department. Advertising and Editorial are undergoing exactly the same reviews so don't feel you're being penalised or being picked on because it's a company-wide review. It's just the state of the current economic climate I'm afraid. It's changing week by week so we've got to pre-empt and adapt if we want to continue to survive when so many titles are going to the wall."

Christ I wanted a fag.

Some people can do that to you; make you want a fag. It doesn't even matter if you've never even smoked before. Five minutes of listening to them waffle on and you're ready to start.

I wanted a fag. I wanted a big, fat, juicy fag.

I wanted to light one end, suck hard on the other and then blow an enormous cloud of hot blue smoke right into Norman's face (and possibly follow it up with a blur of whirling fists).

Check overheads? Current climate? Pre-empt and adapt? All he needed was to call it a challenge and he would've had Bingo.

"… and of course nothing like this is ever easy, but I know you'll give it your best shot and see this as a challenge…" There you go a full house and he'd only been speaking for three minutes. Not too shabby by anyone's standards.

Out of sheer desperation my eyes drifted around his desk

and latched onto the oh so familiar photograph of Norman's never-changing wife. Like Norman's namesake from *Cheers* no one had ever seen his wife, word around the office was that she didn't actually exist, the picture had simply come with the frame. I could quite believe it and even made a point of looking out for her whenever I passed Prontaprint or Snappy Snaps.

"… and this goes right across the board, be merciless, be tough, be decisive…"

Back to the fags. Like I said, I would've loved one but I couldn't. And not just because we weren't allowed to smoke at work any more or because Norman would've frowned upon it or because the shop across the road didn't sell them but because I'd given up six months ago; six months, several days and a few minutes in fact. Fantastic. How great was that? I'd smoked for fourteen glorious years and had enjoyed a modest but regular ten-a-day habit but suddenly all that was behind me. I was a non-smoker once more.

A clean living, non-polluting, fresh air breathing, grown-up, healthy non-smoker. And I would've happily killed every other non-smoker in Britain and climbed across their clean, healthy, cancer-free bodies just to have had one last drag. One tiny, measly, nicotine-packed, deadly, yet delicious drag. God, I would've loved that.

But I couldn't. Because I was a non-smoker again. And non-smokers weren't allowed to smoke. And that was all there was to it.

Somebody had once told me that it got easier with time and like an idiot I had believed them, but it didn't. Or at least, it hadn't. I still wanted one in the morning after my first cup of tea. I wanted one in the car on my way to work. I wanted one during my lunch break and then again at about four. I wanted one at about six on my way home from work. And I wanted a couple in the evening when I sat in my comfortable armchair after dinner and watched a load of rubbish on the telly.

I wanted a cigarette all of these times, every day and more, but most of all I wanted one right now.

"… because that's what being a team player is all about. Are you a team player Andrew? Andrew?"

And perhaps a massive belt of scotch too.

That was something else I was having to cut back on. Alcohol.

I guess it's the same for everyone in their thirties. You cut back and quit, reduce and rethink. I'd spent most of my twenties eating, drinking and smoking whatever had tasted nice to eat, drink and smoke and told myself I'd sort it all out when I got to my thirties. Except who knew how quickly they'd come around?

Don't get me wrong, I'd never been an enormous booze-crazy pill-head like some blokes like to boast they were, but then again by that same token I hadn't exactly been good to myself. I'd enjoyed fry-ups for lunch, chips for dinner, beer in the evenings and fags in-between and had basked in the knowledge that I knew something every jogger in the park didn't – that they were idiots.

I'd been the fittest I was ever going to be in my life and I'd taken it all for granted.

But then I guess most people do when they're young.

Most of us look after our cars better than we do our bodies. My friend Tom bought a new car recently and wouldn't smoke or even pick-up smelly food in it. It was okay for him to constantly stink of fags and battered sausages himself, but he didn't want the same fate to befall his beloved

Volkswagen. Every Sunday he'd be out in the street with the turtle wax buffeting it up to a fine shine and he even missed a medical one time in favour of getting a knocking checked out underneath his bonnet. It's something he still brags about today, but I wonder how much he'll be bragging when that knocking moves to his chest.

Like I say, when you're in your twenties you don't really worry about these things because time's on your side. Heart attack territory is still way off in the distance and the effects of a night's heavy drinking can easily be put right by another night's heavy drinking. It's all a bit of a laugh.

And then one day you wake up, slide your feet into a slightly worn pair of carpet slippers and find a load of birthday cards on the door mat downstairs.

Your hangover lasts a little longer into the weekend, your dinner wipes you out, every ache is terminal cancer and you're absolutely knackered all of the time.

You're thirty.

Or more likely thirty-five.

See, unhealthy living is a heavy old juggernaut to arrest and it ploughs on well into your thirties before you're finally able to get it under control. And what fun it is when you do. I had been on ten fags a day, but now I was on five portions of fruit, two litres of water, thirty minutes of exercise, eight hours of sleep and a couple of minutes of flossing. If that wasn't enough to make a man want to get out of bed in the mornings I didn't know what was.

I'm not the first guy to moan about these things and I don't suppose I'll be the last.

I just wanted a fag that was all.

"… so it's over to you. Make this your number one priority. Go away and take a good hard look at your figures.

Get them down on paper and dissect them until you're down to the bare bones then rebuild them from scratch. I'll want to see justification for the absolutes and alternative solutions for all your other outgoings. Remember, lean and efficient. Make those your watch words and you'll have a very happy publisher on your hands indeed," Norman said, then sat back, folded his arms and took a great big dump in his pants. At least, that's what it looked like from where I was sitting. He was smiling to himself about something and as I'd heard nothing in the last seven minutes that could've possibly caused him to smile, by the process of elimination it had to be the only explanation. Alas I didn't have time to ponder this further as he seemed to be waiting for some sort of a response from me.

Now, given the choice, I would've loved to have seen him prostrate on the floor, with his hands over his ears, wailing like a little girl and utterly broken as a man, but unfortunately my publisher's happiness and the easiness of my working days were index-linked. So I pretended I liked the sound of everything he'd just said and promised prompt action on any number of fronts. This made Norman smile even harder so I made my excuses and got back to my desk before we started ripping the shirts from each other's backs.

"Lean and efficient," he'd said, although as everyone knew this just meant cost cutting. Why then hadn't Norman just said "cost cutting" and saved all the yadda-yadda-yadda?

Simple, Norman liked Norman. He liked his meetings, he liked sounding important at them. He liked wearing a tie and having to put on cufflinks in morning. He liked big words. He liked new words. He liked having a company car. And he liked having the biggest office in the building.

Most of all though, he liked having a staff to share his big new words with.

Don't get me wrong Norman wasn't a bad man by any stretch of the imagination. He'd never been horrible to me or to anyone else for that matter. He always remembered everyone's birthday and never seemed too upset when nobody remembered his. He bought flowers for all the secretaries at Christmas and this year even caught everyone on the hop when he left early on the Friday before the Bank Holiday and said we could all go home too. At least ten of us overtook him on the stairs on the way out.

He did all of these things and more, and yet still it wasn't enough because nobody really liked him.

I couldn't tell you why. I couldn't even tell you why I didn't like him. I just didn't. Perhaps it was because he was in charge and got paid more than me and he'd never once apologised for it. Or perhaps it was because he liked to stick his nose into places he didn't need to stick his nose into and this would always stir up the waters. Either way, he was a fairly uninspiring cricket of a man with files for friends and too much time on his hands. Somebody should've probably taken him out to lunch and talked to him for as long as they could've on as many subjects as they could've just to prove to him there was more to life than work, but that would've meant spending a whole lunchtime with Norman and who could be arsed with that?

Not me.

So I didn't.

And neither did anyone else either.

About the only time I ever really spoke with Norman was when he'd either wander by my cubicle or call me into his office to share a few thoughts on improving the way we did things around here. Naturally, these thoughts would almost always ruin what was left of my day and make getting out of bed the following morning even harder to bear, but this never seemed to faze Norman. He just kept them coming.

His latest idea was a complete break down of my annual budget and a whole justification for each and every individual expense. Where were we getting our pictures from? Could we get them anywhere cheaper? Would it cost less in the short/long term to hire photographers/become photographers ourselves? If not, then okay, but at least we'd looked into these things.

Naturally he wanted all of this in a full glossy presentational report, with coloured pie charts, 3-D graphics, pull-out statistics and cover-mounted free stickers, but just pulling out the costings and compiling the figures for the last year would take a whole day or two. Arguing the case for each and suggesting possible cheaper alternatives would really put the tin hat on it.

What an utter ball ache.

I hadn't even got back to my desk and already I could feel my shoulders sagging with despair as my self-respect packed its bags to leave for the rest of the week. That chap took more time off than the rest of my staff put together.

I slumped into my chair and wondered if I should start right away, but decided I couldn't face it. There was no sense going at it half-cocked, not when I was in this frame of mind, so I file Norman's report in the "crap I'll confront later when I can face it" corner of my brain and spent the next few minutes picking my teeth instead.

Luckily, there was no rush.

Oh it might've seemed like Norman was in a hurry to get things moving but you should never go by other people's time scales. People always ask for everything to be done right away but that's just their way of ensuring they get done eventually. Ask any bin man when he'd like your rubbish out front and you wouldn't be able to get to the shops and back for wheelie bins on the pavement all year round.

So when Norman said, "Make this your number one priority," you have to bear in mind the times we live in and the changing use of language. There's a lot more interpretation these days than there was a century ago. We can't take everything as literal.

For example the following is a short list of my priorities:
Stay alive
Gather food
Maintain a shelter
Look after my wife
Look after my health
Check Lottery numbers every Saturday and Wednesday

As important as it was, I couldn't see myself downgrading any of those priorities in favour of compiling a report on the annual costings of a rather poorly performing caravan magazine. Yes, that's what I do for a living. I'm the editor of *Caravan Enthusiast*, a spectacularly unpopular monthly magazine that covered every conceivable mind-numbing aspect of a dying pursuit. And it couldn't die fast enough as far as I was concerned. I hated them. It's funny, I never used to before I worked on the magazine but then I guess ten years of writing reports on awnings can do that to a man.

God I was bored.

And not just bored, I was frustrated.

When you work somewhere, the importance of the thing you're working on is always exaggerated beyond all proportion. Just take all that throwaway crap that gets stuffed through our letterboxes every day of the week for example.

Flyers, junk mail, loan offers, take-away menus, cab company cards and occasionally, if you're lucky, a free individual packet of washing-up liquid you can stash under your sink in case of an emergency. Somewhere in the world there were people whose days were dedicated to producing this stuff. Can you imagine that? All that crappy, unimportant, nuisance litter that forces you to stoop unnecessarily in the mornings and fills, on average, two extra bin liners per person per year, was actually the focus of some people's working lives. Printers, designers, advertisers, marketeers and their minions. How the hell were we meant to progress as a society with all this going on? Pardon me if I'm wrong but I thought we were all meant to be living on the moon and going to work on jet packs by the year 2000. I specifically remember all that stuff on *Tomorrow's World*; jet packs, robot best friends and a couple of coloured tablets for Sunday lunch. What the hell had happened to that lot? Were we all lied to or did the world just get sidetracked keeping me informed about all the latest Pizza Hut deals?

What am I talking about? I don't know. I guess I'm just bitter and depressed because it had finally sunk in that life was really pretty unimportant. Or at least mine was.

Yeah sure some people were out there somewhere making startling breakthroughs with cancer research, stem cells, nuclear fusion, artificial intelligence, space exploration and, of course, rocket science but most of us were just cluttering up the world with crap and annoying everyone else.

Caravans? I mean, seriously, caravans!

Caravans were things people attached to the backs of their cars once a year so that they could drive down to the seaside and stay in a field. They were cramped, ungainly, lightweight, rickety and cold, and they cost about as much to hire for a week as seven days stay in a rather nice B&B. Though of course, these were just the ones that people attached to the backs of their cars. There were plenty of caravans in the world that never actually went anywhere. They simply rolled out of the factory, found a nice little patch of grass in Weston-Super-Mare and sat there and rusted for the next thirty years.

Like I said, I wasn't against them before I started in this job, but seven years of having to deal with people who thought they were the most precious things on earth, that's what did it for me. Caravan manufacturers, caravan retailers, caravan park owners, and most despicable of all, Caravan Club members.

I wanted the grab each of these cretins by the scruff of the neck every time they phoned to complain about some little mistake we'd printed and drag them off to the nearest paediatric ward and continuously slap them until they were prepared to admit that caravans were simply the things they attached to the backs of their cars to go on holiday in.

I wanted to, but I couldn't, because I was the editor of *Caravan Enthusiast*, and as the editor of *Caravan Enthusiast*, I couldn't very well go around beating up my readership, not if I wanted to continue to gather food, maintain a shelter, look after my wife and buy lottery tickets every Saturday and Wednesday. It simply wasn't possible to do both.

In years gone by I'd been able to take out some of these frustrations on a few strategically timed cigarettes but I couldn't even do this any more.

All I had was my job.

My insignificant, boring, tedious, crappy, little job.

And my report too.

God, I wanted a fag.

Sally's Diary: November 22nd

ANDREW CAME HOME *cursing Norman again. I don't know why he works himself up so much. It's actually quite embarrassing to watch. Also, I can never work out what's so bad about Norman. He doesn't sound too terrible to me and certainly doesn't seem to justify the names Andrew reserves for him. I've tried to pin Andrew down on this point but he just gets annoyed and tells me I don't understand. And he's right, I don't. I don't understand at all. From what I can gather Norman's latest crime is to ask Andrew to draw up a plan of the budget and shave off a little here and there. That doesn't sound too unreasonable to me. After all Norman is Andrew's boss. He is entitled to ask Andrew to do stuff every now and again, isn't he? What does Andrew expect? It's not like he's asked him to work late or take a pay cut or sit on his knee and suck him off. All he's asked him to do is compile a few numbers and write up a report.*

To be honest, I think anything you're asked to do (within reason) during working hours is fair enough. It would be different if Andrew worked in a nineteenth century cotton mill and he was expected to crawl into the machinery to extract his colleagues' hands whenever they clogged up in the gears, but he doesn't.

Andrew works in publishing. How terrible can it be?

I think about Andrew and all his constant complaints then I think about Carol at school. Carol is such a wonderful woman, just turned sixty and still as energetic as a humming bird.

She's really upset she has to retire at the end of the year and almost cried when the children presented her with all the birthday cards they'd made for her in Art. I think she's incredible. She's been at that school since she was in her early twenties, almost forty years, and has taught children of some of the children she taught years ago, which is amazing, and in two or three instances, their grand-children.

But does she have any regrets?

Not a single one. She says she's loved every second of her life and, given the chance, she wouldn't do a thing differently if she had to live her life all over again.

I told this to Andrew and you know what he said?

"Jesus, what a saddo!"

Typical.

But what I wouldn't give to live a life as sad as Carol's.

CHAPTER 2.
SEX LIVES OF THE POORLY PAID AND ANONYMOUS

TIME IS AN amazing thing.

Just trying to get your head around it is all but impossible. Believe me I've tried.

About the only way you can do it is by putting it into some sort of context. The popular way is by condensing the whole of time into a normal 24 hour day. Actually forget that, the whole of time is too big a deal. Let's just condense the lifetime of the Earth into a normal 24 hour day.

Four and a half billion years.

Right, here's what happened.

Earth was formed out of a swirling mass of dust and space particles and at midnight was one big molten horrible place to live. Slowly it started cooling down but it wasn't until about quarter past five in the morning that you could finally take your flip-flops off and run into the sea. If you had've done that, you would've probably found a horrible green film covering just about every rock and pebble. This was the local tenant and an abundant bloke he was too. He had pretty much the whole planet to himself until about six o'clock in the evening when the seas suddenly filled up with hundreds of little monsters that started to eat the green film. Unfortunately for these little monsters bigger and even more horribler monsters came along to start eating them up, so that before you knew it you couldn't turn around without seeing a great big set of teeth chasing you around in circles.

A few of the smaller monsters decided they'd had enough so at ten o'clock that night they crawled out onto the land to escape the carnage. Once there, they found their old green friend again – plant life – enjoying a nice, safe peaceful existence and instantly started eating him again.

By half ten, all the big monsters were now up on the land and the whole feeding frenzy was repeating itself all over again...

Actually, you know what, this is simply too massive a time scale too, so let's forget about when the world formed and concentrate on condensing life's time scale into a 24 hour clock.

Okay, it's midnight again and the seas are just starting to turn green... Actually no, that's still too big a time scale, so let's go back and start it when actual proper, walking about life began.

Six hundred million years ago.

Hmm, you know what, I'm not even going to worry about dinosaurs. The dinosaurs are too huge a lump of history to deal with so let's just talk about man.

Scientists would have us believe that man's been around for a million years (that's about two minutes to midnight on the 24 hour clock) but to be honest if you saw one of these 'men' walking down the street, you'd phone your local zoo to tell them they'd left the gates open again.

No, man as recognisable as man, has only actually been around for about a hundred thousand years.

Okay, so, it's midnight again, we're all dressed in animal furs and Rachel Welsh is back at the cave getting passed around until someone invents the telly. On this time scale, Jesus only showed up at quarter to midnight and the war finished less than fifty seconds ago.

Incredible isn't it, when you think about it? The war, for me, was like another lifetime ago, but in real actual species terms it's not even a minute old. Now that really was amazing.

Time was amazing. Time was precious. And time was always slipping away.

Each of us got such a tiny little fragment of it for ourselves, a razor thin slither of light between two great immensities of blackness and what did we do with it? What did we achieve?

Personally speaking, I'd used rather a lot of mine up trying to work out what time it would've been when the dinosaurs disappeared if the world's history was a 24 hour clock (about half nine I think) when I should've been getting on with Norman's report. It was four o'clock in the afternoon (the real four o'clock) and my desk was buried underneath dozens of Post-it notes, each covered in drawings of clock faces, calculations, cigarettes and Brontosauruses. Or should that be Bronosauri? I spent another ten minutes looking it up on the internet and found to my surprise that it was actually Brontosaurs, which made sense, before turning back to the question of my report.

It was now ten past four and the thought of going through the files had become even less appealing. I'd arrived at work this morning with the intention of having it done by the end of the day but then I'd got sidetracked with all this 24 hour time line business right up until mid-afternoon before realising all I was doing was putting off going through my files.

Miserable defeat sank through my soul as I turned my chair to look at the jumbled bank of filing cabinets and I wondered if there was anything else I could do before I got started.

"Godfrey?" I called across the partition to the opposite cubicle.

[Silence bar the clicking of a mouse]

"Godfrey?"

"What?" Godfrey replied without looking up.

"Want to do me a favour?"

"No."

"What do you mean no? You don't even know what I'm going to ask yet."

"Well I don't know specifics but I know it's going to be something shit otherwise you wouldn't be asking me, you'd be doing it yourself," he reasoned.

This was classic Godfrey. Besides me there were three other people who worked on *Caravan Enthusiast*. Godfrey, my assistant, Elenor, my secretary, and Adam, my designer. Elenor and Adam worked on a couple of other motoring titles too but Godfrey was all mine, although if you were to see us in action you could be forgiven for not knowing which of us was the dog and which of us was the tail.

"I'm busy," I told him.

"Doing what?" Godfrey asked.

"Doing… doing… what does it matter what I'm doing. I am your editor, you know."

"You're not *my* editor. You're the editor of the magazine. I don't have an editor. I am unedited."

"What does that mean?"

"I don't know," he mumbled, before returning to his mouse clicking.

"Godfrey, can you just do me this favour, pleeeeease?"

"Do it yourself."

"Okay fine, if you want to be like that then this is how it is; this is not a favour, this is a direct order. I want you to go through the files and pull out the remittances for every contributor, photographer and freelancer for last year," I told him in no uncertain terms.

"Fuck that!"

"Godfrey, I'm not asking you, I'm telling you," I repeated, in case he'd missed that key detail.

"You can tell me all you want but I ain't doing it. That's a secretary's job. Why don't you get Elenor to do it?" Elenor shot us both a steely look, so I stepped out of the firing line and told Godfrey I didn't want Elenor to do it, I wanted him to do it.

"Why?"

"Why? Why not? Because I do. Because I'm your boss. Because that's my prerogative. Now get on with it."

"What is this, fucking Russia or something? Do this! Do that! Look sharp! *Jawohl!*" he saluted.

"That's German, you moron," Elenor sneered, picking at her split ends.

Godfrey ignored her dig, as he always did, and focused the full glare of his sulk on me.

"I ain't doing it and you can't make me. I'm in the union and I'll phone them up if you try to force me to do that shit," he warned me in no uncertain terms.

"The NUJ aren't going to be interested in your piffling little complaint," I told him. "And besides you told me your membership had lapsed because you hadn't paid your subs."

"I'm still a member. I'm still part of the union. I've still got the card."

"Why does everything have to be a fight with you? Why can't you, just for once, do as I ask?"

"Oh what, so you're asking me again are you? Two seconds ago you were ordering me. One threat of industrial action and suddenly you're only asking me. Just goes to show, doesn't it," he said, giving me his best knowing look over the top of the partition before sinking out of sight again.

"I give up," I resigned, slumping back into my chair. I started rubbing my face out of sheer frustration but before I was all done Godfrey was asking if he could go early.

"You are joking aren't you?" I double-checked.

"No, I've got to go – dentist's appointment. I did tell you about it this morning," he insisted.

"No you didn't," I replied, scouring my memory for any mention of dentists.

"Yes I did. I fucking did. As soon as I got in," Godfrey maintained, already on his feet and in his jacket.

"Oh just go," I told him, too tired for a confrontation. "But I'm going to remember this, I am."

"What, that you let me go to the dentist's? I look forward to reading about it in your memoirs."

I stared at Godfrey as he headed towards the door and savoured several fantasies in which he begged me for his job and I threaten to tear up his P45. Then, seeing as this was a fantasy, I swapped the P45 for a PPK and Godfrey started to bawl.

"Would you like a cup of coffee?" Elenor asked, distracting me just as I was about to put two rounds into Godfrey's imaginary kneecaps.

"What?"

"Coffee? Would you like one?" she repeated. I blinked several times to let this soak in and noticed Godfrey was doing much the same, only with one hand on the door.

"Erm, yes, that would be lovely," I cautiously accepted, watching Elenor watch Godfrey through the back of her head. Godfrey refound his purpose and hurried on to his fictional dentist's appointment, leaving only a swinging door and a bewildered Editor in his wake.

"I'll just be a moment then," Elenor smiled, sauntering off in the direction of the kettle.

I blinked several more times then sank back into my chair with an amused smirk. If you're wondering what was so unusual about Elenor asking if I wanted a cup of coffee, it's because Elenor never made coffee. Never. Never never never. She was a fiery little Fembrandt who bowed to, and made hot drinks for, no man. She'd made this abundantly clear on her first day when I'd accidentally tried to hand her my cup and even the conciliatory offer of several hobnobs wouldn't warm her glare for a couple of days.

Elenor didn't make coffee.

Not for anyone.

Full stop.

"Just because I'm a secretary, it doesn't mean I'm your skivvy, to sit on your knee, flutter my eyelashes and make you coffee," she'd told me several days later when we were finally back on speaking terms. "I'm employed to do a professional job of work, to see over the day to day running of the magazine, organise the admin side and blah blah blah…"

Other stuff came after that but I couldn't tell you what because I'd shut it out in favour of picturing her beautiful curvy little peach resting squarely on my knee.

"I fully understand," I pretended because this seemed like the easiest thing to do.

"I'm glad, because this is the 21st century you know, not the Dark Ages," she'd pointed out, before holstering her glare and dropping her hands away from her hips.

Let me tell you a bit about Elenor. Elenor was a very sexy girl. Some girls needed make-up, clothes, hairspray and bubblegum to look sexy. Elenor just needed Elenor. She wasn't a classically beautiful girl. She didn't have bleached blonde hair, 38DD knockers and legs from here to heaven. It was more her attitude. Elenor knew what Elenor wanted and Elenor usually got it.

She was strong and stern, and as hard as a tank full of tungsten frying pans. I would've hated to ever get on the wrong side of her though the right side must've been a very nice place indeed.

That was often the way with strong women (or girls even); those fires that burned within would erupt to the surface with equal measures of passion, regardless of whether you were rolling around in the hay with them or trying to pass them your coat. Not that I'd known either scenario. My relationship with Elenor was very much like my relationship with Godfrey – cold, frosty, minimalistic and full of resentment and sick days. I was their editor, their boss, the bloke who occasionally asked them to come off the internet to do some work, therefore I was the enemy.

When she'd first started on *Caravan Enthusiast*, she and Godfrey had forged a bond in the face of the common enemy (ie. me). In those days the office had been alive with circumspect whispers, secret jokes and stolen glances, and every word spoken had been flavoured with hidden gibes.

"Oh Godfrey, thank God you're here to keep me sane! If it weren't for you I think I'd go out of my mind with boredom," Elenor would announce, a few feet away from me. "It's soooo boring here. You're not boring though Godfrey, you're a good laugh."

As childish as these little digs were they still used to make me feel self-conscious and I'd end up moping over my own shortcomings before returning to the business of circling my night's telly in the TV guide.

"I saw some firemen on my way home last night. God,

Firemen are soooo sexy. Godfrey, you should be a fireman, you'd look great as a fireman. Girls really like men in uniforms, they're *soooo* sexy. Unlike suits. Urgh, what a turn-off! There's nothing unsexier than a man in a suit. Yuck!" – That was the last time I bought something in Burtons on my lunch break.

This all quickly became tedious on a monumental scale and turned an already crappy job into an all singing, all dancing, daily face-slapping dose of misery.

I hated it. I hated them. But most of all, I just hated. Full stop.

Godfrey in particular seemed to thrive on the whole antagonistic atmosphere and yinged to every one of Elenor's yangs. He became like a wilful teenage boy who back-chatted me at every opportunity and deliberately ate salt and vinegar-soaked fish & chips while I was trying to force down my salad two desks away, though I got the impression he was only being difficult in an effort to impress Elenor. Of course this all pointed to one thing – that he was banging her. But surprisingly few people believed this simply because Elenor was so foxy and Godfrey was so utterly not. It didn't make sense. But then sex often doesn't. Sometimes sex is more about power than attraction and different people often have sex for different reasons. At least, that's what Sally's glossy periodicals reckoned. Watching Elenor and Godfrey at play, if nothing else, confirmed all this coffee break mumbo-jumbo.

Admittedly, I wasn't certain they were having it off, but they sure looked like a couple who were having a clandestine office affair. They went everywhere together and couldn't have a conversation with anyone else without rushing back to report their findings. They bought each other little presents (chocolate bars and sweeties and such like) and wrote each other secret notes. They twittered and tweaked and giggled at things that didn't need twittering, tweaking or giggling at and Elenor even started making Godfrey the occasional cup of coffee. Most of all though, they talked incessantly, on and on and on and on, about everything and nothing – mostly nothing actually – and they almost always agreed with everything the other said. On the rare occasion they didn't see eye to eye, there'd be heated words and heel digging, tantrums and tears and then half a day of heaven-sent silence. This would last until Godfrey worked up the courage to grovel for forgiveness when he thought no one could hear him and before you knew it they'd be super-best friends again.

It was nauseating in the extreme.

I remember thinking at the time that I bloody-well hoped Godfrey was having sex with Elenor because I couldn't see anyone behaving the way he was behaving out of just friendship, so he must've been getting something. Or at least, hoping to get something.

I say this not as a sexist, or a lumbering old fashioned chauvinist or anything, I say this simply as someone who knew Elenor.

She wasn't the nicest person in the world.

Okay, so she was strong and stern and hard and all the rest of it, but you can be strong and stern and hard without being a fucking bitch. Elenor obviously disagreed.

Elenor had, what I believe the Spice Girls used to call, "attitude".

"Nah, she's just a little cunt," my friend Tom, who worked on our sister publication, *Camper Van Magazine*, dismissed. "Take away her tits and the ability to dish out blow-jobs and she wouldn't have a friend in the world." I wasn't sure I agreed with that but I could see his point. She used what God had given her to get what she wanted. And what she had wanted when she'd first started was an office full of soap-opera squabbling to spice up what was effectively a rather hum-drum job.

Me and Godfrey had happily tolerated each other for two years before Elenor walked through the door but the moment she did that all changed. He suddenly became animated in all the wrong departments and I became the hated figurehead of the establishment.

Like I said, it took me a while to come to the conclusion that they were having sex but when I did I started to wonder where they were doing it. They couldn't have been doing it at Elenor's as she still lived with her parents and I doubted Elenor would've travelled all the way back to Godfrey's dingy little bedsit in Balham so that really only left the office.

A rather unsettling thought.

I found myself wondering where specifically they were doing it and finally narrowed it down to the second floor toilets or the back issues stock room, though the key for this door had been lost some time ago so there was no way of doing it in there without the risk of somebody walking in halfway through. I didn't know this from experience, I'd just worked it out one afternoon instead of filling out one of Norman's monthly editor feedback forms.

Of course that was just during office hours. Once we'd all gone home they could've been doing it anywhere. Now this I really found unsettling and it wrinkled my nose every time I arrived in the morning to find my keyboard and stationery all over the place. Again, I couldn't be certain, it might've just been the cleaners (having sex on my desk) but it all added to the whole crapness of my job.

And this is the way it looked like continuing, possibly for the rest of my life, until one glorious morning I came to work to find Godfrey and Elenor weren't talking. They sat there in ear-splitting silence until lunchtime came along and Elenor rushed off to leave Godfrey confused and indecisive. He looked at me and then out of the window then he got his coat and sat back down.

He waited like a dog, staring at the door for Elenor to return, but she didn't, not until two o'clock, and when she did she was laughing and joking gaily with Clive, our cor-blimey full-on Cockney Group Ad Manager.

This stumped Godfrey good and proper and he spent the rest of the afternoon chewing his lip before finally attempting to talk to Elenor last thing. But Elenor wasn't interested: she was "… going out with friends tonight. We're going on the pull. We're right sluts when we get going we are".

I could well believe it and by the look on Godfrey's face so could he. This was no idle bluff either but a genuine open-handed smack right across the chops to knock him for six and Godfrey felt the full force.

He stumbled about almost punch-drunk for a full thirty seconds before collecting his coat, his bag and his wits and heading for the door.

He was late the next day and his eyes were bloodshot and full of booze. Elenor frothed and bubbled with excitement in the seat between us and while she didn't tell us anything directly, we got to hear the whole story as she burned up the company phone bill.

It went something like this:

"Oh no, I can't say anything at the moment. (pause) No I can't. (pause) Oh stop it, behave. Ha ha ha, what are you like! (pause) Now that would be telling. (pause) Hahaha, you dirty bitch, no, I can't. I can't! (pause) Steve. (pause) A kick boxing instructor. (pause) You can say that again, hahahah. (pause) I'll tell you later. (pause) No, I said later. (pause) Because I can't, I'm at work. (pause) Oh, no one special. (pause) Because I… (pause) Ha ha Stacey, you utter tramp, what are you like! (pause) Yeah. (pause) Yeah. (pause with some additional sniggering and a whiney little squeal that built into a screeching crescendo). You know I did, ha ha ha! (pause) His place. (pause) You know what I mean! (pause) Three times. (pause) Ha ha ha, you dirty bitch, of course I did. (pause) Up the arse and in the gob."

Maybe my memory had added that last snippet of detail but either way it was horrible to watch and I had to watch it six times as that's how many girlfriends Elenor chose to phone up in order not to say anything. Godfrey looked absolutely devastated and used up so much energy simply trying to hold it together that, by the afternoon, his shadow was calling the shots.

"Godfrey, do you want to do me a favour? Can you get some money for a Travelcard from accounts and go around all the WHSmiths in central London to see who's stocking our magazine?" I asked, inventing a job just to rescue him from an afternoon of hell.

Godfrey gratefully accepted and drew a tenner from accounts before heading for the nearest pub. Naturally, this also called time on all of Elenor's phone calls and I was able to enjoy a few hours of peace and productivity – a rare treat for me.

Godfrey called in sick the next day and went AWOL the day after that so that it wasn't until Monday when we saw him again, by which time he'd been exposed to a whole weekend of pub advice.

"What's this?" I asked, looking at the envelope he'd just handed me.

"My notice, effective immediately," he informed me.

"Your notice? Why are you giving me your notice?" Godfrey shrugged, though his shrug was surprisingly descriptive. "Have you got another job?"

"No."

"Then what are you going to do?" I asked. Godfrey looked around the office in a way that suggested this particular question hadn't come up on Saturday night.

"I don't know," he said, after some thought.

"Then perhaps you should think about it," I suggested, handing him back his envelope.

"I'll just go on the dole," Godfrey informed me.

"What a loser!" Elenor muttered under her breath to no one in particular.

Godfrey scowled at her for a few intense moments before I got his attention when I told him he wouldn't be able to claim dole for up to six months if he quit of his own accord.

"Have you got enough savings to see you through six months?"

Godfrey didn't. In fact, he didn't have enough savings to buy himself lunch.

"Then what are you going to do? Seriously, think about it. You can't go around handing in your notice when you've got nowhere else to go because that's the sort of thing that can land a man on the street, or worse still back at his parents'."

"I can get another job," Godfrey eventually replied.

"Then get one, and give me this back when you do. In the mean time… why don't we have a cup of coffee? Godfrey?"

Godfrey thought about it for some time then replied "no sugar" and reluctantly retook his seat. Elenor waited for me to ask her if she wanted coffee and when I did, she beamed with glee and told me she took it dark and strong. "Just like my men," she added unnecessarily.

This was four weeks ago and a lot of coffee had passed under the bridge since then, although none of it had been made by Elenor. See Elenor never made coffee. This was just a fact.

She never made coffee. Never never never.

Until today.

When she made a cup for me.

Sally's Diary: December 8th

CAROL'S REALLY excited because the school board say they might be able to find a role for her after she retires. She won't be able to stay on as Head Teacher but they say she'll probably be able to come back on a part-time basis and help out for a few hours a week, maybe even provide sick and holiday cover. Carol's really pleased because she'll be able to get back to actual teaching and forget about all the time-consuming admin that comes with "the nice office". She even said she'd recommend me for the position of Deputy Head if Jenny got her job (as is expected) but I'm not sure I want the extra work and responsibility right now. I'll be thirty-four next year and I'm thinking that perhaps it's time I sat Andrew down and pointed out to him that there are still only two of us in this family.

But you know what, suddenly that particular conversation doesn't seem so daunting.

By some miracle he's no longer slitting his wrists every time I ask him about work. The word "fine" seems to have replaced "just fucking awful" and he's even humming again – always a sure sign of Spring.

I don't know what has happened to bring about this transformation, but then again I never really got to the bottom of what was making his job so terrible in the first place. Andrew's not really one of life's great communicators. All I hope is that whatever it is, it continues for a while and Andrew stays in a good mood for... well, I was going to say the next few months but if I'm wishing for miracles I might as well go for broke and ask for the rest of his life (or at least the rest of mine).

If I didn't know him so well, I'd almost be tempted to venture that he'd been gripped by the Christmas spirit but I know that's not right. Andrew and Saint Nicholas don't make the best of bedfellows and his new-found cheer is sure to be swept away by a tsunami of murderous anger the moment he has to go out Christmas shopping.

I do hope he doesn't get me another engraved pen. There's only so many a girl can accidentally lose.

CHAPTER 3.
SHOP TILL YOU DROP

SOMETHING WEIRD WAS happening. I'd only stepped out for five minutes to make a cup of coffee, but when I got back to the office everyone had gone. Everyone.

I looked at my watch and saw that it was lunchtime, which went some way to explaining this, but it was still weird how there wasn't a single soul left.

Normally, only about half a dozen people off our floor actually go anywhere for lunch; the rest of us make do with a sandwich out of a packet or half of last night's dinner out of a tupperware tub.

This was different though. Everyone was gone.

Everyone.

Somebody must've been having a birthday drink or leaving do that I didn't know about. Or maybe, more likely, the management had finally got around to fine-tuning the fire alarm so that only everyone else in the office and dogs could actually hear it.

I didn't know. All I knew was that everyone was in on something except me.

I thought about calling Godfrey to ask him where he was, but then I didn't want to make it look like I'd been overlooked so I decided to second-guess where they'd all be, grabbed my coat and headed for The Dog & Bull.

When I stepped out of the building however I found Croydon unnervingly quiet. Katherine Street didn't have a single person on it and the air was still and empty. I walked around the corner and saw that Queens Gardens were deserted too. I still wasn't overly alarmed as occasionally they had a bit of a show on in the Whitgift Centre around the corner that sucked all the stragglers from the surrounding area, so I figured this would be where everyone was.

I was just about to head around there myself when I noticed the main road fifty yards away.

It too was dead.

I watched it for several seconds, expecting to see a car come along and break the spell but none did. Not a car, a bike, a lorry or a bus.

The road was empty.

This definitely got my attention and I looked about from east to west, then north to south, for signs of life, but there wasn't a soul to be seen.

I was all alone and horribly confused.

What the hell was happening?

Either a terrorist alert had emptied Croydon or the Pound Shop had just lowered its prices, so I headed off for the Whitgift Centre to see for myself.

Park Street and the High Street were just as deserted as Katherine Street. Rather more disturbingly the pubs on the way around were as dead as doornails. The Rat & Parrot was empty (even by The Rat & Parrot's standards) and the posh pub opposite a shell. I poked my head around the doors of each and both still appeared to be open for business. All the lights were on and all the pumps were glowing. I almost called out for assistance, then thought better of it.

I'd seen those films and no good ever came from calling out.

I left as quietly as I'd entered and hurried along to the Whitgift Centre. Unbelievably, this place was deserted too. I ran from shop to shop and found them all open. I even succumbed to temptation and punched open a cash register to find it stacked full of notes. I pulled them out and folded them up but frowned at the thought of what I was doing.

Should I take it?

The obvious answer was yes, but then if the security cameras were on and I was the only man in Croydon, Surrey police wouldn't have to clock up too many man-hours tracking down the culprit. And did I really want to be that rat that always made the papers after every disaster?

SCUMBAG THIEF LOOTS SHOP WHILE HERO FIREMAN BATTLE TO SAVE THOUSANDS

I always hated that bloke, as did everyone. And he always got his just desserts.

DISASTER THIEF BLUBS IN DOCK AFTER GETTING FOUR YEARS. "HE SHOULD'VE GOT MORE!" DECLARES OWN MUM

Hmm, not tempting.

I put the money back and closed the till. If the population of Croydon were off somewhere being saved, I wanted to be saved with them too, or better still, one of the people who saved them. And if they weren't, then I could always come back for the money later.

I peered out of the shop and saw that the street was still deserted.

I then thought about phoning Sally but realised I'd come out of the office without my mobile. I walked over to a public phone and picked up the receiver but there was no dialling tone. What's more, I could hear somebody grunting on the other end of the line. Or maybe chewing.

"Hello? Excuse me," I said.

"*Uh! Uh! Whoozat?*"

"Hello, who is this?"

The voice thought for a moment then asked me a simple question back.

"*Where are you?*"

I thought better of answering him, put down the phone and stepped back a few paces.

I didn't like this. I didn't like this one little bit. I screwed up my face as the fear tightened my innards and thought about crying, but it had been so long since I'd last cried that I'd forgotten how to.

I had to get out of here. That was all there was to it. I had to get to my car, put my foot down and get the hell out of here. Something was wrong. I didn't know what. I only knew I didn't want to hang around and find out the particulars.

I was just about to run back when a noise stopped me in my tracks. It was way off in the distance and I had to put an ear to the wind to hear it, but when I did I liked my situation even less.

It was a wailing. Or more accurately, it was lots and lots and lots of wailing. And it was getting closer.

I turned away from the wailing and began to run but only made it a few steps when I realised I was running in the direction of the wailing. I turned back and ran the other way but the sound was coming from that direction too. In fact, the sound was coming from everywhere and it filled the air with noise.

All at once I saw the first of them. He stumbled into view at the end of the street then began staggering in my direction. He looked like he was drunk but I soon realised he wasn't drunk – he was dead.

But he was walking?

Okay, so he was one of those walking dead mateys? Big deal, live and let live, now let's get the hell out of here, I told myself, but the other way was already blocked.

More dead. More walking. More wailing.

The Whitgift Centre was suddenly alive with those creatures and the doors of the Drummond Centre opposite began swinging backwards and forwards as walking corpse after walking corpse spilled out on to the High Street.

"Oh fucking nora," was all I could think to say.

I had hoped my last words on Earth might've been a little bit more profound than "Oh fucking nora!" but they matched the occasion beautifully so I decided to go with them.

The faces of the dead were pale and blue. Some looked as though they had died horribly, whereas others looked like they had died in their sleep. One or two looked like they had only just clawed their way out of the ground, which was where I guessed all this had begun. It didn't really matter. They were here now and they were all around me.

It was too late to run, too late to hide. Even if I'd tried to bolt they would've been onto me in a flash. All I could do was stand very very still and hope they didn't notice me.

So that's what I did. I stood very still in the middle of the High Street and barely dared to breathe.

The dead mingled and milled, knocked into each other and even me, although incredibly none of them afforded me as much as a glance. I was just another obstacle to them, no more or less interesting than that tree some fat zombie had just wandered into therefore I was invisible.

I was just starting to think I might even get away with this when one of the zombies stopped in her tracks and turned straight at me.

"Are you okay, Andrew?" the zombie asked.

I blinked a couple of times and saw Elenor looking at me curiously.

"Are you alright?"

"What? Oh yes. Yeah fine. Just miles away, daydreaming," I shrugged, and looked back at the fat zombie to see that he'd turned into a fat businessman. He was rubbing his head from where he'd walked into the tree and frowning down at the slice of pizza he'd just dropped.

"You looked lost," Elenor pointed out.

"I am really. Christmas shopping. I never know what to get. I always just end up thinking about other things," I explained, *Dawn of the Dead* from the night before providing today's inspiration.

"Who are you buying for?"

"Sally. My wife," I told her.

"What does she want?" Elenor asked.

"That's the point, I don't know."

"What would she like?"

"I don't know," I shrugged once more, as if it were going out of fashion.

"Well, what did you get her last year?"

"A pen. It was a nice silver one. It was engraved with her name and everything. It was nice."

"Sounds great," she smirked sarcastically. "Did she like it?" I thought for a moment and admitted I didn't know that either. "Then you should probably steer clear of pens in the future," Elenor advised.

"She makes it so difficult. Every year I ask her what she wants and every year she says the same thing; 'Don't get me anything too expensive, just get me something little.' But like what? What's little and inexpensive and still nice that I can buy without feeling like a bleeding tightwad? Do you know of anything?"

Elenor said she didn't but ventured it was the thought that counted.

"I know, and that's the annoying thing. I hate shopping and Sally knows it and she knows I haven't got a clue what to get her and yet she deliberately engineers a situation where I have to put a bit of thought into what I get her."

"The cow!" Elenor tutted.

"Oh you know what I mean. I've been wandering around these shops half the lunch hour and I haven't found a single thing she'd like," I complained. "How many more hours am I going to have to spend traipsing around the shops just because she won't let me throw money at the problem?"

"Why don't you get her some nice underwear?" Elenor winked.

"What, some pants?"

"No, not some pants, some nice underwear. Some sexy underwear. Could be fun for both of you."

"I don't think so," I dismissed.

"Why not?"

"Sally's not really the sexy underwear type."

"Why, what's she got, udders or something?"

"What, no. I just mean, I don't think she'd like sexy underwear…"

"… as much as a pen," Elenor finished for me.

"No. Well yes. No. I don't know."

"I think sexy underwear would be a brilliant present," Elenor said, and I liked the way she kept saying sexy underwear. It was sexy. "I'd be thrilled to bits if somebody bought me a nice pair of see-through lacy panties and a matching see-through bra," she told me, raising an eyebrow provocatively. "Absolutely thrilled to bits."

"Would you?" I laughed nervously, but Elenor didn't respond. "Well, you never know, maybe Santa will bring you some in your Christmas stocking."

"If he does, he'll leave my house with more than a mince pie and a glass of sherry," she promised before wishing me luck with my search.

I watched Elenor walk off into the crowd and gave her a wave when she looked back.

At that moment all the zombies returned, although Elenor just walked right through them. It was incredible how none of them noticed her. Not one of them. How could they not notice her? How could anyone not notice her –

– in her see-through lacy panties and matching see-through bra?

Sally's Diary: December 25th

ANOTHER CHRISTMAS Day over. Boy, Christmas Day really is the Sunday to end all Sundays isn't it? Personally, I've always preferred Christmas Eve. Christmas Eve for me is the best day of the year, the Friday to end all Fridays. I've always enjoyed Christmas Eve yet rarely enjoyed Christmas Day. I don't know why this should be. Perhaps it's because Christmas Eve is all about preparation, hope and anticipation. Even the travel is something I enjoy. The roads are calm, the air's tinged with expectation and the journey's like the start of a mini adventure.

Then you arrive, climb out of the car and suddenly you remember you're staying with your parents for the next few days.

Maybe the reason Christmas Eve is so magical is because it's the calm before the storm. It lulls you into a false sense of security and makes you believe that this year it might be different. But it never is. God, Jesus, Buddha, Allah, Mohammed and anyone else I've forgotten to mention, please, I pray to you with every ounce of my soul don't let me turn out to be like my mother.

In other news, Andrew excelled himself this year by getting me a painting by numbers kit. I can't help but wonder why.

I know he's not the best at buying presents but still…

Every year he tried to bludgeon me into telling him what I want for Christmas, but what I want is a surprise. Something thoughtful. Something little. Something nice. That's what I want. I don't know what it is myself, but that's the whole point. All I know is that it's not an engraved pen, it's not a foot stool, it's not a self-operated back massager and it's not a painting by numbers kit.

Is this me being difficult? I hope not. I'd hate to think of myself as a difficult person. All I really want is a little surprise (not that the painting by numbers kit didn't catch me by surprise).

We do both sets of parents in quick succession every year, Andrew's first on Christmas Eve and Christmas morning, then my parents afterwards for Christmas Day evening and Boxing Day. In years gone by, we used to wrap each other's presents up again so that we could 'unwrap' them in front of both sets of parents but we decided not to bother with that this year. I'm glad. I found it hard enough pretending to be thrilled to bits with a painting by numbers kit once as it was.

I'm not sure I could manage twice.

CHAPTER 4.
MOTORWAY MADNESS

MY REARVIEW MIRROR flashed a couple of times and I looked up to see a BMW almost on my tail lights. I was in the outside lane of the M3 and moving along at a respectable 79mph. The two inside lanes were moderately busy with cars and lorries so I was overtaking the slower 60mph and 70mph traffic myself, but BMW man had obviously come to the conclusion that this wasn't fast enough for an expensive car like his so he was giving me a taster of his front lights and badgering me to get out of the way.

I normally have no qualms about getting out of the way of other motorists if I'm blocking the fast or middle lanes of the motorway, but this doesn't happen very often because I only ever use the middle or outside lanes for overtaking. When I'm cruising along daydreaming about my dinner I stick to the furthest inside lane and only pull out to overtake caravans, buses, lorries, coaches and Fiats, then I steer straight back in again when the road up ahead is once against clear. This is what you're meant to do. This is how you're meant to drive on a motorway. I know this because I passed a test in order to get my driving licence.

BMW man had obviously found his in a fucking Christmas cracker.

"What?" I asked the rear view mirror as it flashed me once again.

"Hmm?" Sally asked, stirring in the passenger seat beside me. She rubbed the sleep from her eyes and looked out of the window. "Where are we? What's up?"

"Oh nothing, it's just this… *what, you fucking fuck?*" I yelled, as a wall of light filled the back windscreen.

"Andrew!" Sally exclaimed, shocked at the outburst. I don't normally swear, especially not in front of Sally, but I do sometimes resort to it in moments of extreme stress.

Here is a list of things that will make me swear:
Smacking my head
Hitting my hand with a hammer
Stubbing my toe on the corner of the bed in the middle of the night
Catching a falling cactus
Seeing some sort of monster running towards me
Self-assembly instructions
Sally's parents
Christmas shopping
Norman
Other drivers

If I had the road to myself, or if everyone just stuck to the rules and we all drove like we were supposed to, then I could scrub that last one off my list, but there were so many wankers on the road that I burned to turn my car into an instrument of death every time I got behind the wheel.

"You son of a fucking…" I growled, putting my foot down to get the arsehole off my bumper.

"Andrew, What's wrong?" Sally asked, looking over her shoulder as my speedometer needle checked out the view from the 80mphs.

"It's this fucking arsehole on my arse," I told her. "He keeps flashing me and…"

Pharp!

"You bastard…!!!"

"Andrew!"

"Well he just hooted me."

The cunt!

"What does he want?" Sally asked.

"He wants to get past," I told her.

"Well let him," she said, unbelievably.

Pharp! Pharp! Pharp!

"MOTHERFUCKER!" I screamed, almost snapping the steering wheel off in my hands.

"Andrew, just let him past!"

"But I'm not doing anything wrong," I explained.

"What the hell's that got to do with anything?" Sally asked, but I was too busy steering into a long sweeping curve and watching for gaps in the traffic to answer her.

"Andrew, just pull in so that he can get past," she insisted.

"But I'm doing eighty miles an hour already," I said, then saw I wasn't, I was actually doing 92mph. 92mph and he was still only ten feet off my bumper. What was the matter with this maniac?

"Andrew!" Sally snapped, but I'd be fucked if I was pulling in for him just because this arsehole wanted to hare along on his own private road at 100mph.

I'd been doing 79mph as it was. The national speed limit's 70mph but this fucking dickhead had flashed and beeped to overtake me when I was overtaking traffic myself. You know it's one thing to speed when you have a clear stretch of road ahead of you, but it's quite another when you have to intimidate other speeders in order to do it.

No, bollocks to him! I wasn't getting out of his way. I was in the right and I had the law on my side. At least, I would have once I'd shed 22mph.

Accordingly, I eased my foot off the accelerator and slowed to a comparatively snail-like 73mph.

The stupid thing was that I would've probably pulled over and let him past if he had just sat in my rear view mirror and bided his time, but it was the fact that he'd tried to bully me off the road that got my goat up. Why should I have to slow down and get out of the way for him just because he had a faster car than me? Why should I? Who did he think he was? And why the *fuck* did he think that counted for anything with me?

BMW man began wearing out his horn and strobing the back of my car but he could go fuck himself as far as I was concerned. I was Gandalf of the M3 and he was not passing.

"For Chrissakes Andrew, just pull the bloody car over and let him past!" Sally yelled, but I refused to budge from the outside lane and explained that it would be wrong of me to knowingly allow someone else to break the law, "like that arsehole behind me. I mean, if I was on a train and he got on and told me to beat it because he wanted to touch up all the female passengers, should I turn a blind-eye and let him do what he wanted or stay and try to protect them?" I asked, congratulating myself for coming up with such a fitting analogy.

"What are you talking about, Andrew? The only female passenger around here in any peril is me because you're playing bloody motorway cat and mouse," she pointed out, then yelled in my ear, "Now bloody well pull in before you get us both killed!"

Sally was gripping the handles of the seat and bracing herself for a pile-up although we were only going at 73mph and I was in total control.

"Sally, it's all right, don't worry, we're not going to crash," I reassured her. We were now entering a long straight, the road was dry and the weather was clear, though this cut little ice with Sally who was adamant I was about to kill everyone within a five-mile radius.

"Fine, stop the car. Stop it. I want to get out and walk," she suddenly demanded.

"Don't be so silly."

"It's not me being silly, it's you who's being silly, playing with my life as if this is some sort of game. Now stop the car, I'm getting out."

"I can't stop, it's a motorway."

"Stop the car!"

"He's the one playing games, not me," I insisted, but it was no use. I was in the one in the wrong. Again. As far as Sally was concerned, I was always the one in the wrong.

"Stop – the – car!"

"Fine, have it your way, I'll pull in but he's the one who's going to crash and blow up five miles down the road," I told her.

"Would you rather he did it in the back of us?" Sally asked, but I was no longer listening, I was dipping my indicator lever and slowing down to pull in between a Volkswagen Polo and an old Ford Focus.

It felt oddly humiliating having to pull over and let this arsehole win, like everyone else on the motorway was looking at each other and smirking, and I wanted Sally to lean out of the passenger side and explain to the rest of the traffic that I was only letting him past because she'd told me to, but that wasn't going to happen any time soon.

I eased into the middle lane and thought that would be it, but BMW man roared alongside me and sat there waiting for me to turn and look at him. Curiosity finally got the better of me and when I turned I saw a scrunched up face and five clenched fingers yelling and shaking in my direction.

I wound down the window and held a hand to my ear so BMW man did the same and called me a "wanker", a "cunt", a "fucking tosser", a "wanker" again and "David Blunkett" in an impressively short space of time.

"You want to learn to drive mate, you shouldn't be on the fucking road!" I yelled back.

"Wi.. ou. . n… ckin… ..up …. … . .g. … ou… nt!" he replied.

"Yeah, well have some of that," I shouted, and gave him the finger.

"… ll… kin… . sh .. ur.. d. up.. . .. ntin.. .. nt!" he retorted, and performed a complicated 'one-finger, wanker-sign, one-finger, fist' routine while holding his car perfectly level with mine.

"You're gay!" I told him.

"Oh for God's sake Andrew," Sally complained.

Beethoven in the BMW put his hand to his ear, so I repeated it several times and did a John Inman hand flap and pointed in his direction, so he came back with a few gestures of his own.

"What's he doing now?" Sally asked.

"I don't know," I told her, charades not being my strong suit. "Maybe he's hungry."

"Just ignore him, Andrew," Sally told me, though I felt strangely drawn to watch a bit more, and only wound the window back up when he tried to throw an empty coffee cup at me.

Naturally, the polystyrene vessel didn't get within two feet of my car but it still panicked me into winding up the window. When I looked back, matey was laughing and giving me the V-sign, so I quickly wound my window back down and called him a "fucking moron"!

"Quick, have we got anything to throw?" I asked Sally, but Sally refused to join in and once again asked to be dropped off on the hard shoulder.

"Fine," I conceded, then wound my window back up despite BMW man's continuing gestures to concentrate on the road ahead.

When he finally got the message I was no longer playing, BMW man did the same and zoomed off into the distance with a final roar of indignation.

"You're all the bloody same, aren't you?" Sally observed, before crossing her arms and turning up the silence.

I was in no mood for a fight so I left it at that, though it annoyed me how little faith she'd shown in me. Like I'd said, it was a dry and clear day, we were driving along a long straight motorway at a safe and legal(ish) speed and I'd had the rules of the road on my side. What did she want me to do? Give way to everyone else just because they'd forgotten the Highway Code and apologise for being there in the first place? Christ on a bike!

You know what, you should never let yourself get pushed around in life. Weakness only ever led to more pushing around. Sometimes you had to push back, even if it meant taking a fist in the face. It's not fair and it's not fun but sometimes it was the only way. This was the price we all paid for being men. An X and a Y chromosome and bike with a crossbar simply didn't cut it. Men had to *act* like men, not just look like them. What was it Kipling had said? Something about exceedingly good cakes? I can't remember. The point is men weren't born. Boys were born. Men were something we had to become.

This is a concept Sally never understood.

"Don't say anything."

"Turn the other cheek."

"Don't get involved."

"Just look away."

"Don't forget to thank them when they've kicked you in the teeth."

That was pretty much Sally's philosophy of how I should behave.

Well that wasn't my way. And it wasn't BMW man's way either, but Sally had stuck her oar into something she couldn't comprehend which meant that BMW man got away with it and now he was off laughing at me. It was microscopic; barely a slither of a fraction of a percentage, but thanks to BMW man's aggression and Sally's fear, the world had become an ever-so slightly worse place to live.

Christ I wanted a fag.

I couldn't blame Sally for how she'd reacted because Sally was just being Sally, and Sally had to be true to herself. It was more the hypocrisy that annoyed me. I mean, how would she have reacted if some little kid in her class had started painting all over the walls and every time she'd tried to stop him I'd told her to turn the other cheek?

Who would be in the wrong then?

Me of course. It would always be me.

It was annoying and it was infuriating but what could I do? Sit her down, explain the situation to her and hope she eventually saw reason? Or give up and simply say "yes Sally", "no Sally" and "three bags full Sally"?

Which held the greater promise of a peaceful life for me?

Singletons might think it would be the former; the sit her down and talk to her option, to get an open and frank dialogue going, but every time I've tried that in the past, the open and frank dialogue almost always got quickly hijacked and I'd have to listen to her dragging my self-esteem through six dozen different hedgerows for about two hours while she got everything off her chest.

No talking rarely worked. All talking ever really did was wake you up to the fact that you had ten times more problems than you ever dreamed of.

With this in mind, Sally and I sat in silence stewing over the same incident from different perspectives while a cold and wintry Surrey slipped by at an icy lick.

This was a real pity actually because we'd got on brilliantly over Christmas, better than we'd got on in years and I'd really been looking forward to getting away from the folks and spending some quiet time with just Sally at home. Now that looked to have gone for a toss with the BMW incident, which would no doubt hang in the air for the rest of the day and flavour every glance and remark.

"Shall I put on the radio?" I asked, but Sally didn't answer.

I did so anyway, in the hope that a familiar song might soften both our moods, but all I had to show after five minutes of continuous tuning were Car Phone Warehouse adverts and euphoric DJs boasting about how drunk they'd got over Christmas, so I turned it off again and played "count the red cars" with myself for twenty minutes or so until I almost crashed out of sheer despair.

"Shall we stop at the Services?" I suggested, spotting a sign for Fleet Services.

"Why?"

I didn't know. We had loads of petrol and neither of us were particularly hungry or needed the loo. I just thought it might've been good.

I liked motorway service stations. They were unusual places that you only ever visited when you were on long journeys somewhere and that didn't happen very often, at least not to me it didn't. I always thought of them as little islands in the sea, with tea and cake and light bulb-baked sausages, where ships passed in the night and truck drivers washed their armpits. There was also something slightly rough and ready about them that I liked, due no doubt to the fact that they were pretty much inaccessible except by motorway so that they weren't full of annoying teens or cheerful pleasure seekers. Everybody in them was just passing through. Actually, forget the little islands, they were more like border towns, or no, better still space ports or something. Nobody talked to anyone else, nobody mingled, they just had their bacon and eggs and coffee and washes and contemplated the things that waited for them many miles away.

"We could stretch our legs."

"But we're almost home," Sally pointed out.

This much was true. We were now only about four miles from home and due to take the next turning so there really wasn't any reason to go to the Services.

"We could pop in anyway if you liked," I said, but Sally wasn't keen.

"Let's just get home shall we?" she said, and that was that. We passed the Services without slowing and I felt the pang of regret at the lost opportunity.

"I might give Tom a call when we get home. See if he wants to go out for a drink tonight," I said, causing Sally to glare at me all at once.

"I thought we were going to have a quiet night in?"

I was half-tempted to tell her that I wasn't sure I fancied it this quiet, but I figured that would only fan the flames of this particular disagreement so I settled for looking bewildered.

"When did I say that?" I asked.

"Oh whatever. Go out if you want then, I don't care," she

snarled, so I deliberately missed the subtext and played along as if I'd just been given the green light.

"Great," I beamed, letting her know my emotional blinkers were on and that I could no longer read between the lines. I was pretty confident I'd get away with it too, because Sally hated putting her objections into actual words, so as long as I was prepared to pay the price (ie. two days of short shrift) then I'd get to have a couple of pints tonight.

And believe me, I was.

Well you might as well get hanged for a lamb as a sniff of the barmaid's apron, as they say on the internet – somewhere probably.

I was just wondering how early I dared make a break for the pub when brake lights started filling the horizon. The traffic immediately thickened and before I knew it I was working my way through the gears and down to first. A few hundred cars tightened up to a crawl and all too inevitably we ground to a halt.

"Oh, what is this now?" I moaned, winding down the window and craning my head out when I saw some guy in front do something similar. I couldn't see anything but then again neither could he, so we both ducked back into our cars and speculated with our respective partners as to what the problem could be.

"It's probably a crash," Sally said, underlining those few carefully considered words with a tone that didn't make it past my emotional blinkers.

"Well I hope it's nothing serious, we're only half a mile from our turning."

We sat in the same spot for another thirty frustrating minutes before a gradual trickle of movement started shifting cars from our view. I started up the engine and waited expectantly for the movement to reach us and when it did a clear stretch of motorway, roughly the size of a family saloon, opened up in front of us. I drove straight into it. And then another bit of motorway opened up and so I drove into that one too and so on until three lanes merged into one and we circumvented a twisted heap of steel and glass that looked like it used to be several different cars. Astonishingly, no bits looked like they used to be attached to a BMW, which meant my finger-waving friend had been stuck in this same mess along with the rest of us, no doubt flashing his lights and hooting his horn at the logjam in front of him. Ambulance men and policemen were already on the scene and doing their best to clear the road and keep the traffic moving, though the wreckage was strewn right across three lanes, so we were having to be directed onto the hard shoulder.

The cars were already empty and I wondered how their occupants had faired. One of the wrecks looked as though it could've been walked away from, though I doubted the same could've been said of the Vauxhall Corsa wrapped around the central reservation barrier. That one was a mess. A tin can crushed to bits by rampaging elephants.

"I hope they're okay," Sally said, looking past me as I steered my way around the accident.

"Yeah, me too," I agreed, though I didn't hold out much hope.

All at once the traffic cones and police tape ended and the motorway opened up in front of us again. I moved through the gears up to fourth, and then fifth, but stayed under 60mph for the last half a mile. Other cars sped past me like a hail of bullets but I wasn't interested in keeping pace with them any more. The turning for Camberley soon appeared, so I checked my mirrors and pressed down the indicator, signalling an end to mine and Sally's motorway adventure.

To tell the truth, it hadn't been the best car journey of our lives.

But at least it hadn't been the last.

Sally's Diary: December 27th

THE RELIEF *at being home again is tempered by yet another little niggling row. Andrew and I don't have blazing rows. I wish we did because I bet they're easier to patch up than our niggling ones. With niggling rows they're almost always over something that's so tiny, so petty that neither of us want to talk them through for fear of being thought of as tiny and petty ourselves. So what do we do to do? Well, I usually bite my tongue and try to keep the peace, but this rarely works as the niggling just ends up hanging in the air, drifting from one day to the next. I hate niggling rows, I really do, but they seem to just keep coming out of nowhere. Last week's happened because Norman bought Andrew a bottle of wine for Christmas. Seriously, Norman got him a present, a lovely bottle of sparkling wine and told him to enjoy it with his Christmas dinner and Andrew launched into a rant about how it was some devious move to try and buy his respect. "Of course, now I've got to buy him something and how he'd like that, hey!" he fumed, working himself up into one.*

Andrew's not really one to listen to anyone when he's in that sort of mood and he ended up roping me into his bad temper when I refused to condemn Norman for his gift (although he soon held out his glass when I cracked it open that evening). Silly, isn't it?

Today we niggled over... over what? Some insane petulant nonsense on the motorway. God, why does he always have to be right about every little thing? Some other driver behind us wanted to get past and Andrew wouldn't let him. It was like some sort of game to him. Ridiculous, isn't it? It really is. In fact, as I'm sat here writing this, I can't even understand how it all blew up again. Why couldn't he just pull over? There you go, problem solved, next problem please. I mean, if he's going to fall to pieces every time something this tiny inconveniences him, how the hell's he ever going to cope if something serious goes wrong? And you know what, that's my real frustration. I work with children all day long. I'm getting a little bit tired of having to come home to one.

CHAPTER 5.
THE GREEN GREEN GRASS OF TOM

"THIS BASTARD WAS right up my arse; hooting and trying to flash me off the road. I tell you, some people," I said, draining the last of my pint.

"Blimey, you thirsty or something?" Tom asked, half a pint behind me.

"First one I've had since… well, before Christmas I think."

"Really, you haven't had anything at all over Christmas?"

"No, just scotch and wine."

Tom angled his eyebrows. "That counts. I thought you meant you hadn't had any booze, full stop."

"Oh no, God no. Three days at mine and Sally's parents? Christ, I couldn't do that sober," I shuddered.

"Go on then, what did matey do?"

"Well, he was just there wasn't he, hanging off my arse and trying to intimidate me into the central reservation."

"Cunt!"

"Yeah, that's right. He was like a maniac he was, a total fucking nutcase. I thought he was going to kill someone."

"So what did you do?"

"Well I wasn't going to let him past, was I, so I let the bastard stew."

Tom gave a considered nod and took the penultimate sip of his pint. "In your own time, Tom," I said, nudging his arm along.

"What? Oh yeah, sorry," said Tom, downing the dregs and summoning the barman away from his *Take a Break* magazine.

"Same again, Tom?" the barman asked, hovering a couple of fresh glasses under the John Smiths.

"Please Graham. And have one for yourself?"

"Thanks. I'll have it for later, yeah?"

"No problem," Tom nodded, all pleased with himself at being so flash. Still, that was Tom and Tom liked being flash. He wasn't flash in a 'in-your-face' 'Jack-the-lad' 'utter-wanker' sort of way. It was more a languid, unconcerned, look at me, aren't I cool, sort of thing. I was never sure where he got it from, whether it was Clint Eastwood in *The Good, The Bad and The Ugly*, Michael Caine in *Alfie*, or Regan out of *The Sweeney* but he'd definitely got it from somewhere because when I first met him he couldn't even open a door without knocking his glasses off.

Still, he seemed to enjoy doing it and it also seemed to work too, so I stopped pulling him up on it whenever I caught him smoking out of the corner of his mouth or winking when he thought he'd said something clever, and let him just get on with it these days.

"So what's Sally's problem?"

"Oh, I don't know. You know her, she's always upset about something. I can't seem to do anything right these days." I took a big gulp of my new pint, wiped the bubbles from my top lip and let that sentiment have some time by itself.

"Probably her period or something I suspect. That's usually what's the matter," Tom guessed, making the barman roll his eyes.

"No, I don't know. Maybe it was all a bit stupid but it wasn't my fault. I didn't do anything wrong."

"Ah, women they don't understand these things. It's just easier to blame stuff on their blokes because they're the ones at hand. Try doing something to a bird that they don't like and see how much they like it," Tom winked.

I met Tom at University. In fact, that's where I'd met Sally too. She'd been in the year below us both, but we'd all worked on, or at least contributed to, the University paper, so we'd ended up getting to know each other. This was also how me and Tom had started in journalism and how I'd ended up on *Caravan Enthusiast* and Tom had ended up on *Camper Van Magazine* (Sally saw mine and Tom's dreadful career fates and immediately took the decision to do something useful with her life, sparing herself forty-odd years of media tedium).

Oddly, if a little unsettlingly, Sally had dated Tom before me for about a week or so before realising [Sally's words] "what a dreadful mistake I was making" and [Tom's words] "dropping me like a hot turd." I've never understood how a woman can like a bloke enough to go out with them, see them two or three times and even sleep with them (as happened on this occasion), only to then realise what an utter dork they are and chuck them? I've never understood this.

"Come on, you have to admit, he is a bit of a knob," she once said.

"Well you fucked him darling," I unwisely retorted.

I've often wondered what went on the night Sally realised her "dreadful mistake" because it was one specific particular night, but neither of them have ever talked about it so I don't suppose I'll ever know. I'm certainly never going to ask. The curiosity did occasionally grip me, but what if I found out they'd worn each other's pants or spanked each other with hair brushes?

Then again perhaps it was nothing. Perhaps it was nothing at all. After all they were both young, naïve and inexperienced at the time, so how deranged could've things got? Perhaps Sally just woke up the next morning, rolled over and thought,

"So this is what hitting rock bottom feels like is it?" or perhaps she just figured she could do better. I like to believe the latter as it flatters me at the same time, though I reckon the real reason's probably something a bit more embarrassing because Tom's never talked about it either.

"So, is she in a big sulk with you then is she?" Tom asked, taking three attempts to flick a fag into his mouth before finally succeeding.

"No, it's nothing. I'll just keep my head down and it'll be fine in a day or so. It's just annoying that everything's always my fault. I just wish one day she'd support me, I mean, I thought that was what marriage was all about – two people supporting each other."

"Really? Who gave you that idea, Gandhi?" he winked.

"Stop doing that."

"Despite everything everyone says these days, women actually just want to be looked after. That's the way it's always been and that's the way it'll always be. The blokes do the giving, the women do the needing," Tom sermonised.

"You don't half talk a load of rubbish sometimes."

"Believe what you like, but you tell me this; you're always going on about this argument with Sally or that argument with Sally but when was the last time she admitted she was wrong about something and said sorry?"

"I don't know," I shrugged, doing a quick Ctrl + F on my memory but coming up short.

"So when was the last time you did it?" he then asked.

"Well, tonight obviously," I admitted.

"And the time before that?"

"I don't know, just before Christmas, I guess."

"And the time before that?"

"A few weeks earlier probably."

"And the time before that?"

"Is your record stuck?"

"I'm just making a point here," Tom said.

"Which is?"

"Which is, we're the ones who have to do all the supporting, not women. We support them, we look after them, and we're the ones who have to shoulder all the blame whenever anything goes wrong. That's what being a man is all about. That's where the expression comes from, being a man," Tom nodded knowingly, pausing to take a man-sized swig of his pint before continuing. "Men have to hold their hands up, take it on the chin and not grumble. If I said to you, my dad went to the doctors, was told he had three weeks to live and took it like a big woman, you'd know exactly what I meant, wouldn't you?"

Images of Tom's dad bawling on the doctor's carpet, begging and offering sexual favours for medicine filled my head, so I said, "yeah, sure".

"Now, if I told you he went to the doctors, was told he had three weeks to live and took it like a man, what would you say to that?"

Tom's dad got up from the carpet, wiped his eyes and laughed manfully.

"Three weeks to live you say? Why that's just grand. Gives me time to play golf every day and blow Tom's inheritance on hookers. Fancy a sneaky pint before I tee off?"

"Hence, being a man calls for certain characteristics and being a woman calls for other characteristics. That's just the way it is," Tom concluded.

"You know, the scary thing is you really believe all of this, don't you?" I said, finishing my next pint before I even knew about it.

"I'm sure I won't win any awards at the next PC rally, but everything I've said is true. Men are men. Women are women. You just have to decide which you want to be."

Tom didn't wink, although he looked as though he wanted to, but three winks in as many minutes would've seriously devalued the gesture, so he settled for nodding sagely and saving his next wink for something spectacular.

"And what's all this 'we' and 'us' bit? Last time I checked you were still single. If you know so much about it, how comes you haven't got a girlfriend?"

"For precisely that reason, because I know so much about it," he winked, unable to resist the lure of that one. "Besides, I do all right."

This was annoyingly true. Tom did, indeed, do all right. Every few Mondays he'd have some tawdry tale of bedroom bingo to share with me and it wasn't all bullshit either. Some of it obviously was, but not all of it.

Take for example his last conquest – Su Li is the name on her birth certificate but she's since become better known as "that little Chinese bird I'm banging". Tom showed me a picture of her a little while ago (clothes on, obviously) and she looked absolutely fantastic: as pale as a drop of snow and just as palm-meltingly delicate.

"Dirty as fuck, she is too. Wanked me off in the taxi and let me do it all up her face when we got home."

Now, I have no doubt he was bedding this "little Chinese bird" but I couldn't believe the details because they simply didn't tie in with my experience of girls.

I mean, sure, yeah, there were probably some girls out there who did these sorts of things, but let's be honest, they were going to be pretty few and far between. And I'm not talking just about sex on a first date here either; that would be refreshingly restrained if only I were. No, I'm talking about nasty porno-type dirty things that you only read about in the sleaziest (ie. the best) sex magazines – bondage, threesomes, lesbianism, doing it in public, doing it up the bottom, all that sort of thing. If Tom were to be believed, practically every girl in the world (or at least in Britain and China) was an insatiable dirty nymphomaniac who's only concern in life was getting it as hard as she humanly could.

Now, like I say, obviously some of this was bullshit but not all of it.

See, the reason I believed most of what Tom told me was because Tom used to be hopeless as far as girls were concerned, absolutely hopeless. And this is something he freely admits. He didn't have a clue. Every Friday and Saturday night he'd polish his glasses and head out with his best Ben Sherman on, but the only thing he'd ever pull would be a kebab on the way home. And that's the way it went for Tom. That's the way it went for him for a very long time in fact.

Eighteen months was his longest stint without sex. Can you imagine that? Eighteen months?

In those last few months he became really quite hopelessly pathetic; a cross between a manic depressive and a strung out junkie.

Lesser men would've given up, cut it off and turned gay/ serial killer/train spotter if they'd had to go through what Tom had gone through, but not Tom. No he stuck it out, determined they weren't going to get the better of him and kept banging his head against a brick wall until he finally managed to con some poor naïve 24-year-old into taking her bra off in front of him. Tina was her name, and an equally hapless and hopeless specimen of insecurity you couldn't wish to take advantage of. Tom dated her at arm's length for about four months before leapfrogging into the bed of another girl and dumping Tina 21st Century style, ie. with an email. The email had been short, sweet and to the point. Here's what it had said:

> *Hi Tina,*
> *Sorry for not calling back this weekend but I've been really busy. Also, I've been thinking and I don't think it's working out. Hope you understand but I think it's best if we cooled it for a while. Take care, and good luck at the dentists, I'm sure it'll be fine so don't keep worrying.*
> *T*
> *ps. I posted you back your Greatest Love Songs CD but I think I sent it to the wrong address.*

I printed this off and showed it to Sally simply because I couldn't believe it.

I also couldn't understand why he'd done this to Tina, especially after all he'd gone through himself, but Tom just said that it was his turn to be a bastard.

Well, from that day onwards it seemed permanently Tom's turn to be a bastard, because the next girl went the same way, as did the girl after that and the girl after that.

Tom's confidence grew with every weekend and he even started winking at people whenever he said something clever and suddenly he was the bee's knees as far as girls went. He still didn't have any luck finding any sort of long-term soul mate but as far as [Tom's words] "old bikes up against bus shelters" went, he had it all sewn up.

Naturally, not every girl fell for his charms, an awful lot actively despised his guts in fact, but he laughed at his failures as well as his successes, so I reasoned a lot of what he told me had to be true.

"You dumped Su Li?" I said, Tom having told me this while I was telling you about him. "Why?"

"Well, she weren't all that to be honest. Too many teeth and not enough tits, if you know what I mean."

I didn't.

"Why did you go out with her then?"

"What d'you mean? You saw her. Why wouldn't I?" he said.

"Well I don't know. Perhaps if you didn't actually like her or couldn't see a future in it," I argued.

"Yeah well, I'm not like you, am I? I just like sex."

"What are you talking about, I like sex," I objected, loud enough to draw a shout of, "get a room" from the back of the pub.

"No, you don't like sex, you like having sex with Sally and there's a difference. I'm talking about sex; sex for the sake of sex. A big pair of tits and a neatly cropped fanny and some bird who's name I can't remember lying there and letting me do whatever I want alongside her. That's what I'm talking about. Just tits and fannies."

"And they say romance is dead."

"No it's not dead, it just has nothing to do with sex, that's all," Tom said, taking a puff on his fag and blowing several smoke rings across the bar. "Don't get me wrong, I think you're the luckiest bloke in the world. You've got a cracker of a wife you're in love with, a happy and stable marriage and a couple of kids limbering up in her ovaries. I reckon you've got the lot."

"And so will you if you keep on shagging around like this," I told him.

"Oh no, don't worry, I'm always safe. I mean, you have to be really these days, don't you? Not fair on the bird," he said, with uncharacteristic consideration. "Besides, if you get some disease, you know you have to contact all your old partners and get them to go for a check-up as well. Can you imagine? Christ, there's fifty-seven phone calls I wouldn't want to have to make."

"Fifty-seven!" I exclaimed.

"Yeah, give or take. I lost count around about thirty but I think it's sort of around that mark," Tom pondered.

"Fuck me Tom!"

"Make that fifty-eight," he winked.

"That's loads," I pointed out.

"Not really," he disputed. "Higher than average I suppose, but most blokes have had about twenty birds or so they say." I didn't offer up anything more to this as my total fell well short of twenty and left Tom to consider this one for himself.

"Fifty-seven. Is that a lot? I don't know, maybe. Still, there weren't exactly a lot of quality in there."

"That's incredibly generous of you to say so," I told him.

"I know this one bloke, Martin is his name, drinks in the Duke of York – you met him that one time – he reckons he's shagged over two hundred birds. Can you imagine that?"

"And has he?" I asked.

"I wouldn't be surprised as he is one of these blokes who's annoyingly natural when it comes to women. You should see him at closing time, they're practically hanging off of him, I tell you." Two hundred? Jesus, that was fifty times the women I'd had and one of my total would've been subject to a steward's enquiry.

"I expect this Martin would think I'm the luckiest bloke in the world too," I said.

"I doubt it. He's married an'all," Tom reckoned.

"So when's he had time to shag all these girls then?" I asked.

"What are you talking about, he's still shagging them. Bit bad to be honest. I mean not phoning some bird after you've chucked her pants out of the window, or bullshitting that you're an airline pilot in order to chuck her pants out of the window is one thing, but shagging another hundred and eighty birds after you've walked Miss Number Twenty Five down the aisle is a bit above and beyond if you know what I mean," Tom frowned.

"How the hell's he get away with it?" That's what I wanted to know.

"Fuck knows. Maybe his wife don't mind. Maybe she turns a blind eye. I mean, he might be banging every old boiler in Camberley but she's the one he comes home to every night, or at least most nights, that sort of madness," Tom figured. "And besides, they've got a kiddy too and women always go off sex after they have kids."

"Do they?"

"Oh yeah, that's well known that is. They've done studies on it and everything," he said, presumably to show me he was now talking facts here – not just pub bollocks.

I thought about this when I went to the toilet and concluded it was a load of codswallop. I mean, women not wanting sex after they'd had kids? Dirty birds on every street corner? A twenty girl national average? And Martin from the Duke of York up to his nuts in sluts?

How could any of this be true?

I definitely wasn't sure about the twenty-girl average. In order for that to make mathematical sense girls had to have a twenty bloke average too then, unless of course it was all down to a handful of old boilers with incalculable totals and broken beds?

Sally hadn't had twenty blokes and none of her friends had either. I knew this as we'd discussed it a few months before our wedding.

Sally had slept with only five guys in total, annoyingly two more than me. I'd only slept with three (girls not guys – and this included Sally herself) though I'd once enjoyed a spot of foreplay with a French girl on a campsite and had quickly drafted her into my total when Sally told me she'd had five.

So Sally was well below the national average too.

At least, she was if she'd told me the truth and I can only assume she'd told me the truth as she'd never lied to me about this sort of thing before, but it was possible, I suppose. Everything was possible.

Maybe she'd had more than five men. Maybe she'd even had ten. Or twenty. Or thirty.

If she had've done, it probably wouldn't have been the sort of thing she would've shared with her eager young husband-to-be, especially when that poor near-virgin still had two fingers and a whole other hand free after totting up his total.

Maybe she was still at it. Maybe she was like Martin from the Duke of York and had been getting pummelled senseless by two hundred guys while I'd been at work.

I doubted it, because Sally wasn't the type, but then again who was? You read about these sorts of thing in the Sunday papers all the time and I'm sure these women's husbands didn't think they were the type either, but it goes on.

Hmm.

Elenor?

Now she most definitely the type.

I wondered how many guys she'd slept with and concluded it was more likely to be nearer Martin's total than mine. I thought about her for a while and inadvertently ended up picturing her buffeting and bashing, moaning and thrashing, sweaty, crying, yelping, sighing, stroking, coaxing and sucking her way through an army of hairy-backed gorillas.

Loving it she was. Absolutely loving it.

When the last of them was done, she lay there puffing and panting and doodling her fingers all over her sweat-streaked skin before suddenly noticing me.

"Enjoy the show?" she asked, making no attempt to cover herself up.

I looked down before zipping myself up and realised I had – a little too much if I'm honest.

Sally's Diary: December 31st

IT'S NEW YEAR'S Eve, out with the old and in with the new. I'm going to make a real conscious effort to stop bickering with Andrew and just get on with him. I don't think it's me a lot of the time, but it takes two to argue, just as it takes two to do most things in life, so I'm going to redouble my efforts and hope this inspires Andrew to redouble his. To be honest we're not at each other's throats the whole time. Reading back through my diary you might think we are, but actually most of the time we're perfectly happy. Well, maybe happy's putting it a bit strong. We're together and we're content. To be happy would probably require something else, so I'll start with content and see where I can take it.

Other resolutions: to cut out the chocolate for the whole of January, and to stop watching so much nonsense on the television.

Naturally Andrew's talking up the gym again but for once I've decided not to fall for it. Sure it would be lovely to go to the gym three times a week, take a couple of years off my butt and fit into my old jeans again (I still have them somewhere for motivational purposes) but I think it's time we stopped kidding ourselves. This isn't going to happen. For either of us. Why? Okay, I'll admit it even if Andrew won't. The gym is sooooooo boring. I can't even begin to describe it. I've come to dread January because every January means another two or three weeks of huffing and puffing on a treadmill or a bike or a step machine before we're ready to admit defeat and put ourselves through the ritual humiliation of cancelling our membership again.

Well I've had it. I'm going to finally throw my old jeans away and accept once and for all that this is the shape God intends me to be.

Hey, you know what, I think I've just taken that first step towards that happiness I was talking about.

CHAPTER 6.
NEW YEAR, SAME OLD STORY

THE CROWD WAS on its feet. They could scarcely believe what they were seeing. This unknown, unseeded, last minute qualifier had made it all the way through to the final and he was matching the undefeated six-times world champion application for application.

"Quiet please, ladies and gentlemen. Quiet!" the umpire insisted and an expectant hush descended upon the hundred-thousand-strong crowd that had literally (or do I mean metaphorically?) shoehorned itself into the new Wembley Stadium for this showpiece final.

"Mr Nolan, you may proceed."

I took a few deep breaths to calm my nerves, wiped some of the sweat from my fingertips and gripped the mouse. On screen the cursor hovered over StuffIt Expander and I moved it micrometers to the left and right before finding the exact perfect spot.

"Go for it," I told myself, said a little prayer and double-clicked.

The computer blinked a couple of times then the cursor turned into a tiny clock. The second hand of the clock spun around and around and the crowd rippled with apprehension.

"Quiet please ladies and gentlemen. Quiet!" the umpire urged them again, but it was no use, the tension was just too great.

All at once the menu bar of my Mac went white and StuffIt Expander appeared. I could scarcely believe it but my machine continued to click, whirl and crunch and eventually StuffIt Expander moved across to the right hand corner of the menu bar and offered me a choice of File, iSupport and Help.

The crowd went mental.

The cheering and screaming was almost ear-splitting and it took a good couple of minutes for the umpire to get on top of them again, and when he did, he totted up the number of applications I had opened and found I held the new world record.

Thirty-three applications.

Unbelievable.

The application menu bar almost stretched all the way down the screen and I held it open to admire my accomplishment, as the judges declared me the new Application Opening World Champion.

QuarkExpress, Word, QuickTime, PictureViewer, Outlook, Internet Explorer, iTunes, Adobe, Acrobat, Netscape, RealPlayer, FlashPlayer and so on and so on thirty-three times. They were all open and active. What an accomplishment! Of course, a number of the applications were admittedly pretty small; Stickies and Mac Solitaire, for example, were only around about 100k each, but then that was what made Application Opening such a tactical sport.

"Morning Andrew, I wondered if you had a moment?" Norman said behind me, shitting the life out of me.

I knocked several stacks of papers flying as I tried to click the applications menu closed again but the cursor just turned into a little clock and froze halfway round.

"What's the matter, crashed again? Hmm, yeah, looks like you've probably got too many applications open," he pointed out.

"Er yeah, yeah, I reckon," I agreed, quickly reaching behind my computer and pressing the restart button.

"I know it's the first day back after Christmas and everything so I don't want to rock your boat, but I just wondered if you'd had a chance to do that report," he asked, draining me to my very soul.

That report? Jesus, was he still going on about that? It had hardly been mentioned at all during December so I'd figured I'd got away with it, but suddenly he wanted it again? This was unbelievable. Of course he didn't really want it. He was only asking for it to put me on the spot because I hadn't done it when everyone else had.

For fuck's sake!

This was beyond unbelievable. It was just plain petty and it immediately ruined what I'd hoped was going be a nice easy day.

"Oh, er, no, I'm afraid not, Norman. I took all the erm… files home and everything, to take a look at, you know, over Christmas, but, er…" I clicked, whirled and crunched as my iExcuses application opened up behind my eyes. "But, the thing was…"

Norman frowned and watched the little clocks spinning in my eyes as he resigned himself to hearing what the thing was.

Here were my options.

I took the wrong set of files home?
We got a dog for Christmas and he ate my report?
I left it on the bus?
A dog ate it, possibly on the bus?
What report?
I couldn't be arsed?
Why don't you just fuck off?
Sally's been ill?

Shit, yeah, that was a good one.

"Sally's been ill."

"Oh, I'm very sorry to hear that. Nothing serious I hope."

"No, no," I reassured him then quickly amended that before he asked me why I hadn't done my report then. "Well yeah actually. On and off, you know. I've been run off my feet and pretty worried, to be honest."

"Oh no, she's all right isn't she?" Norman fretted.

"Oh, yeah, fine. She's okay now. Just pretty ill then," I told him, as I tried to express as much unspoken manly concern as I could without inviting too many awkward and unanswerable questions.

"What was the matter with her?"

Like that one.

"The doctors weren't sure. They think it was just a virus, but it pretty much laid her out for the whole of Christmas," I said, desperately trying to shake him off the scent. I didn't want to go into specifics and start talking about symptoms and rashes and lumps and that sort of thing as I didn't feel particularly comfortable steering my excuse through these sorts of waters but fortunately Norman didn't press.

"Is she okay now?"

"As a daisy. I think we both just need some exercise. We're joining the gym on Friday so that should sort us both out," I reassured him.

"Well, please pass on my best and tell her to take care. These things can sometimes reoccur," he said, handing me repeat rights for this particular excuse on a silver platter.

*

The rest of the day ticked along quietly, as work days have a tendency to do, and most people spent it trying to remember what they'd been doing when they'd tossed their files over their shoulders twelve care-free days earlier. Godfrey put himself fairly and squarely in charge of clearing away every last residue of Christmas and even used a wet paper towel to clean the fake snow off the corners of our windows that Rosemary had sprayed last year.

"Oh leave it, it looks nice," Rosemary said when she wandered around and saw him wiping away her handiwork.

"… mumble mumble fucking Christmas mumble…" was all I could make out of his reply and to be honest I had to agree. If there was one thing I couldn't stand it was a never-ending Christmas. I liked there to be a definite cut-off point, a "that's it, all over, unplug the fairy lights and chuck away the cards," followed by a nice quiet, drab January to help straighten out the routine. Consequently, I wasn't looking forward to next week's office Christmas party.

Our MD had decided it would be fun to have it on January 13th to give us a bit of a treat in what was traditionally a rather depressing month, though cynics might've raised an eyebrow and wondered how much Joe Bananas cost to hire in January compared to December. Either way, no matter how much tinsel Godfrey ripped down we hadn't got rid of it yet.

Another constant reminder of Christmas was Elenor's endless partying stories. She'd sung her own praises all morning down the telephone to whomever she could think to call and now it was my turn to get chapter and verse. They were pretty tedious, naturally, but I found myself hanging on her every word. It helped that she'd come around and sat in my cubicle, twisting gently in the swivel chair a mere two feet from mine and pulling down the hem of her tight lycra skirt every time it threatened to divulge its secrets.

"It was amazing," she laughed, at something that sounded an amazingly long way away from amazing. "I mean, we must have been mad. How can you drink eight jelly shots?"

"I don't know, one after the other?" Godfrey suggested

from the other side of the partition, having been subjected to the same anecdotes as me, only with none of the knee entertainment to keep him interested.

That was the thing about Elenor's stories. Up close and personal they were strangely enchanting. Move them back a few feet and point them at someone else and they lost all their appeal.

"What's the matter Godfrey, stay in on New Year's Eve with *Casablanca* and a bottle of red wine again?" Elenor asked, slapping the smirk clean off his face. Godfrey stared at her in stunned outrage, before throwing himself back into his window-scraping. "Ooops, I seem to have touched a nerve," Elenor winked, making me feel rather grubby at being party to such an obvious betrayal of trust.

Still, this tiny little triumph had Elenor positively glowing and her rays were giving me goosebumps all over.

"Anyway, what was I saying? Oh yeah, well, me and Stacey were the last to leave and still dancing our heads off when all the lights came on. It was absolutely mental and the nightclub owner thought we were off our head so he asked if we wanted to stay behind and party with the crew. And these guys really knew how to party, if you know what I mean?" she giggled. I didn't, so I took that to mean her and Stacey got bummed by a load of off-duty bouncers. "God it was mad," she squealed.

"I had a fairly quiet one myself," I told her. "Me and Sally…"

"Oh you should've come up to Croydon, you would've loved it, it was wicked," she enthused. "Just wait till you see me at the Christmas party, then you'll see what I'm really like."

As it happened, I already knew what she was really like

and told her I probably wouldn't be going to the Christmas party. Elenor looked at me as if I'd just told her I worked here for free.

"Yeah, right," she said after a moment. "*Me neither*."

"No, seriously I probably won't."

"Of course you are."

"No, genuinely, I'm seriously not," I insisted.

Elenor pulled this one apart and tried to work out what I was saying, so I reiterated that I wasn't joking. This wasn't a joke. I was being serious.

Her expression changed from one of scepticism to outright abhorrence.

"Why the fuck not?" she finally asked.

"Well, for one thing, I don't want a Christmas party in the middle of January. Christmas is over. I just want to get on with it, not spend the whole year walking around in a paper hat looking for the back of a conga to grab hold of."

"It's free drink isn't it, what's up with you?" Elenor asked.

"What, in this company. Not likely. I think we had a free bar until nine o'clock last year then it was normal prices."

"Half eight," Godfrey corrected me.

"Well that's alright, you can get well pissed in a couple of hours and spend the rest of the night dancing your arse off," Elenor said, swinging her shoulders and waving her arms above her head as she swivelled in her seat to some funky, silent beat.

"I don't think so," I said.

"Why not, what's the matter with you? Don't be boring or you'll end up turning into Godfrey?" she said, catching the full force of Godfrey's glare. "Go on, come to the party," she demanded. "It'll be fun."

I couldn't work out why she was so bothered about what I

did or didn't do. I mean, what difference did it make to her whether I went to this party or not? There'd still be the same amount of booze and food and music and enforced jollity no matter what I did, so why did she need me?

"Go on, we'll have fun," she said, and I couldn't help but notice how "*it'll* be fun" had suddenly changed to "*we'll* have fun".

"I can't. Besides I live all the way down in Camberley, so I couldn't drink anyway," I told her.

"You could get a hotel room," she suggested, looking me straight in the eye and giving me an unexpected hot flush.

I could feel my face burning and my heart thumping heavily inside my chest but Elenor continued to hold my stare. What exactly was she suggesting? Did I have this right, or were my wires more crossed than Albanian Telecom's? No, it couldn't be. All Elenor was doing was suggesting a solution to me not being able to drink. That's all. If it had been Godfrey or Tom who'd suggested it, would I have read them the same way and assumed they'd been planning on bunking with me and planting kisses up and down the length of my sweaty, naked body all night long?

Possibly…

… if they'd been leaning as close to me as Elenor had. Close enough that I could see down their tops and smell their hot sweet breath on my face.

<u>Sally's Diary: January 7th</u>

I THINK THE first *of my New Year's resolution is paying off. Andrew's chipper as a woodchuck with a fresh pile of logs and we haven't had a single row all year. Not even a squabble. Predictably, he's joined the gym again, though he's let me off this year and reckons he's happy going by himself. Tonight's his first night so he's out of my hair for the evening — and Celebrity Big Brother's back on at nine! No, I mustn't. I did promise myself. But then, I've been working all week and January's such a depressing month that you have to allow yourself some little rewards, don't you? Andrew's got his Christmas party next week and he says he might go after all, so I should have something to look forward to, surely? I guess it would be okay if I just watched the Friday episodes and didn't have any chocolate. But then, how can you watch Celebrity Big Brother without chocolate? Hmm, I fear my second and third New Year's resolutions are coming unstuck at the seams. Still, at least I still have the first. And out of the three, happiness, chocolate and Big Brother, I'd say that happiness is definitely the most important one.*

CHAPTER 7.
THE END OF FOREVER

I WAS THINKING about time again. I don't know if this is a proper theory but I'm not sure that time is linear. Do you know what I mean? I'll try and explain. See, when most people think of time, they think of it as just one constant, continuous… erm, well, for want of a better word, thing. It started at the beginning of the universe and will run in a straight line at a set speed until the end of forever – if there is such a thing as the end of forever. And then you've got us and we are simply somewhere along that straight line, as was Churchill, Shakespeare, Julius Caesar, Joe Bloggs, caveman Ug and that chicken I had for dinner last night. Only they've all had their time and no longer exist.

Or do they?

I mean, just because they don't exist in my time any more, might they still exist in their own? Not every creature on God's sunny Earth looks at the clock in the morning through my eyes so it might be possible.

See, just because it's half past ten on a Monday morning, January 10th, early in the 21st Century, today's a bit cloudy and Godfrey's off sick again where I am, that doesn't necessarily mean that it's half past ten, Monday January 10th for everyone, does it? As far as caveman Ug's concerned, it's probably a sunny day somewhere in the Stone Age and he's just broken the tip off his spear chucking it at a wall painting of an elephant again. He doesn't know me and I don't know him, so why should time be measured from my perspective?

Let me put it another way; Shakespeare doesn't know he's dead. Just as Space Captain Jack Laser from the future doesn't know he hasn't been born yet. Just as I didn't know I hadn't been born yet in Shakespeare's time, and probably won't know I'm dead when Jack Laser's buzzing around space battling face huggers.

All I can see is the window of my own life.

So, since I was born I've seen thirty five years so far, so if it's the same for Mr Shakespeare, then surely it follows that for him it's only 1599, Queen Elizabeth is still on the throne and he's looking through a big pot of red quills and wondering where all his black ones keep getting to.

But what if our windows didn't reflect on a single linear time line? What if there were an infinitive number of time lines all side by side, and each of them simply stretched as far as each of our own individual lives? Would it then be possible to jump from line to line? Will I still exist as a thirty-five year-old in my own time line in the future? Or do we just go around and around? The moment we die, we're born again at the beginning? For all eternity?

I didn't know. But I bet whatever the answer is, it's a lot more complicated than I could've ever got my head around.

Also I bet we never find out, just as Shakespeare and Churchill and Ug never found out.

Perhaps you just have to do the best you can with your life and live for the moment, because the moment is so fleeting that it's gone and history before you even realise it.

I looked back along my own particular time line and wondered how much of it I was happy with. Not as much as I should've been I concluded. But then, wasn't that the same for everyone? Okay, so I didn't have a bad life, so there wasn't really anything that wrong with me. I wasn't ill, I wasn't disabled, I wasn't illiterate or destitute or homeless. I wasn't hooked on heroin, struggling to raise five kids single-handedly, mourning the loss of a murdered loved one or trapped on a downed submarine fighting off mysterious deep water aliens with dwindling ammunition. Though that last one might've been good…

"Nolan, we've got to go! They're breaking in through the hull again!"

"You go. I'm staying!"

"Don't be a fool, they'll eat you alive just like they did the rest of the crew."

"I said I'm staying, Tom, now get the hell out of here. Go on, go."

"It's too late, they're through. Oh Christ no!"

"Open fire!"

"Lend us a fiver."

"What?"

"I forgot my wallet and I want to get a bacon sandwich off the sandwich man."

Tom's torn and blood streaked submariner's uniform had morphed into his favourite *I drink therefore I am… drunk!* T-shirt and the navigation console we'd leapt behind to dodge the merciless slashing bio-mechanical claws was now my cubicle again.

"A fiver?"

"Actually make that a tenner. I think I'll have a couple of pints at lunchtime. You're up for a drink aren't you?"

"It's Monday."

"All the more reason."

"No, I've got to do Norman's bleeding report."

"What, you still haven't done it?"

"I've been busy."

Tom looked at the doodles of cavemen, time lines, monsters and cigarettes that were dotted around my desk and said he could see that for himself.

"Here, take this," I said, pulling out my wallet and handing him a twenty. "You'll have to give me the change, it's all I've got."

"Fucking sandwich man's going to love me giving him a twenty," Tom frowned.

"Well what's he want, the exact change all the time? Hasn't he ever heard of going to the bank?"

"You want anything?"

"No, just my change."

"I'll see what I can do. Oh, and give us a look at your *Guardian* too?"

"You want the paper or just the jobs bit?"

"Jobs. Anything in it?"

"Yeah, half the ink from my red pen. You have a go."

"Ta."

Tom retreated to his desk with my twenty and my Guardian and waited for 'sandwich man' to arrive.

The deep water aliens were patrolling the bottom of the sea again, but I'd escaped back to Croydon and was once again wondering where it had all gone wrong? Well to be honest, it hadn't, so why the hell did I feel so disillusioned on an almost daily basis? I didn't know. There was nothing I could really put my finger on so I decided to spend a little more time looking for answers.

My childhood had been okay. A bit boring and uneventful perhaps but I couldn't remember ever being truly unhappy – except when we had to have our cat put down. I hadn't been bullied, and I hadn't been deprived. My parents were still together and no over-friendly ice cream men had ever managed to get me into the backs of their vans so I had no grounds for complaint.

But then by that same token, I couldn't remember

anything amazing happening either.

I'd never really been good or interested in anything, except perhaps art, but I'd never been encouraged to pursue it. My parents were pretty much straight down the line as far as parenting was concerned. As long as we washed our necks, went to school, did our homework and went to bed when we were told to, they were happy to get on with their lives and let us get on with ours. We all had dinners together and all watched the same programmes on the telly but then only one cook in the house and four channels on the TV couldn't help but bring a family together.

Okay so my childhood wasn't all cuddles and kisses and trips to Alton Towers. Who cares? Most people's weren't, so I wound the tape forwards a few years and checked over my adolescence, but there was nothing to write home about there either so I wound it forwards some more.

University I'd liked.

This had actually come as something of a surprise to me, as I hadn't expected to like it. See, for me (and my brother) university was always just something we'd been expected to go to when we'd finished school. We had no say in it and didn't even realise there was an alternative. We just had to get our A Levels and go. In all honesty, I'd just expected it to be another form of school but on arriving, I found it had something that school didn't – absolutely no sign of my parents.

It also had girls, lots and lots of them.

Of course there'd been girls at my Secondary school, but by and large the really pretty ones had been as thick as two short planks and interested solely in blokes who dragged their brains around in their fists and got tattoos when they should've been getting GCSEs.

And those guys weren't here either!

They were all still in that little town I'd left behind, laying bricks, getting drunk and biting each other's ears off at closing time.

It was fantastic.

At university, I could suddenly drop my guard and stand out, and not worry about someone flushing the confident smile off my face as their mates threw my bag onto the roof of A Block. I was happy.

And things went from good to great in my second year.

A very pretty, funny, smart girl on the student paper amazingly didn't throw up all over my shoes when I said hello to her, and soon I was saying hello to her all over campus.

Her name was Sally, and she left me excited, nervous, nauseous, humble, horny and ever so slightly disappointed with myself whenever I thought about her – which was all of the time.

My nausea quickly ballooned into a sickening ball of misery when I'd heard she'd agreed to go out with my so-called backstabbing Judas bastard of a best mate Tom, and I thought my whole soul would rip from my chest and run off down the road in floods of tears when I found out they'd spent the night together, but curiously something was up.

The student paper newsroom was suddenly a rather uncomfortable place to be, Sally and Tom turned carbon-based life-form on each other, and all at once she was available again. As I said earlier, I didn't know what went on and didn't really care. All I knew was Sally was available again and that was good enough for me.

I spent the next few days agonising over whether to charge in there like a preposterously eager rhinoceros before anyone else had the chance to or whether to sit back and play it cool.

While I was weighing up my options, Sally called around and asked me if I wanted to go for a drink.

Yes. Yes I did. The answer to that question was yes.

I could scarcely believe my luck, though I quickly holstered my enthusiasm on the way down to the student union, reasoning that she was actually probably only asking me out as a friend, and not as a potential life partner, taking the pressure off the evening a tad. As it turned out, I was right, though this took none of the shine off the evening. It was a really lovely night and we enjoyed quite a few more like it until one morning, about two months down the line, I woke up with Sally's head on my shoulder and everything had changed. We were no longer simply friends. We were boyfriend and girlfriend, and we ratified this shift in our relationship with three months of the most fantastic sex I've ever known. It was truly wonderful, and I knew at that moment she was the girl for me and that we were destined to be together forever, though I kept this to myself as I figured few things startled a girl quite like an untimely marriage proposal.

No, I bided my time, enjoyed what we had and made the most of the best girl in the world.

Without wishing to be crude, the sex couldn't have come a moment too soon. I was pulling my hair out in lumps, and desiccating myself to a husk just thinking about Sally up in my room, though again this was something I kept to myself.

See the previous year I'd had an on-off-off-off-on-off-off-off relationship with a rather neurotic girl called Natalie who flitted between knocking on my door at midnight and calling me a bastard at all other times, but since the start of my second year I hadn't had so much as a kiss off the cat.

I was frantic – unbelievably frantic. Consequently Sally

copped the back-end of a famine that had me putting in performances Casanova could've hung his hat on. She still occasionally mentions them with fondness today, though like Shakespeare and Caveman Ug they're long gone.

Rather frustratingly, at the time of my drought, about four weeks before me and Sally finally got together, I had an interesting offer from a girl called Abigail. Abigail was something else, as trendy students have a tendency to say. Very sweet. Very sexy. And very vivacious.

She also always used to wear a hat, even indoors, which confused a lot of people back then.

Still, wacky attention seeking dress-sense aside, she was a fiery girl who made little secret of her love of life. Several of my friends shagged her and Tom told me he'd heard she was "filthy as a pig" – in a complimentary sense you understand. And it didn't exactly take much either. If she took a shine to you, she would give you an unmistakeable look and you'd both be away. A dark corner in the Union, the university toilets, occasionally even a bed. Anywhere that was handy really.

And I know what this unmistakeable look looked like, because one night, I found it looking at me.

It came after an all-day session in the Student Union, which followed the handing in of a particularly awful assignment. Me, Tom, Abigail, and half a dozen others decided to bunk off our afternoon lecture and were soon full of beer and bravado at how rebellious we were being. It was actually a brilliant afternoon, almost perfect in fact; the sort of afternoon that you can never repeat, no matter how many times you round up the same faces and force beer down their throats because it was simply a spontaneous one-off. I, myself, was Johnny Personality and had everyone in stitches for hours on end, particularly the increasingly adorable Abigail. She even shifted around to sit next to me and we laughed, whispered and play-poked each other under the table until I suddenly noticed her hand in my lap.

"My, aren't we a big boy?" she whispered, squeezing me in the most wonderful way. "I like big boys, the bigger the better."

She pulled down my zip and slipped her hand inside then asked if I wanted to come to the toilet to fuck. Those were her exact words, by the way. "Do you want to come to the toilet to fuck?"

Honestly, that's what she'd said. No one had ever said anything that shocking to me before and no one's ever said anything that shocking since. Not even Norman. .

I couldn't believe it.

Mind you, if I couldn't believe that, try and imagine how she must've felt when she heard my reply.

"Er, no. It's okay. I might laugh and joke about these sorts of things, but I'm really not like that."

What?

Seriously, that's what I'd told her. I must've been off my chump. What was I thinking? I'll tell you what I was thinking, I was thinking that I was all loved up with Sally and didn't want to blow my chance with her by banging Jack the Hat. It didn't matter that I wasn't actually going out with Sally at the time, or that it had been more than six months since nutty Natalie had last knocked on my door, I just couldn't go with any old girl when my heart belonged to another.

"Go on," she whispered, increasing her grip in an effort to wrestle me into submission, but I couldn't do it, so I eased her out of my trousers, made my apologies and went and played pool with Tom. I guess Abigail wasn't the sort of girl who was used to getting rejected because she left for another pub shortly afterwards and never spoke to me again.

Where to start?

Did I regret turning down Abigail all those years ago?

I didn't at the time, especially when me and Sally finally got it together, but a few years later I remembered the incident and couldn't understand why I'd done what I'd done. I mean, what an idiot!

"I'm sorry but I'm not like that?" I'd said. Not like what? Not like the sort of guy who has exciting guilt-free sex while he's young and single with a sexy girl who's "filthy as a pig"?

I reiterate I must've been off my fucking chump.

I also can't begin to describe to you how many times I've kicked myself for not dragging her into the bog and driving her through several cubicle walls. I really, *really* have. And it wouldn't have affected my burgeoning relationship with Sally because I doubt she would've even heard about it. And if she had, what difference would it have made? She'd been with several guys and had even gone on a couple of dates while we were 'just friends', so it wouldn't have made a penny's worth of difference.

In fact, the only thing it would've done would've been to even up our personal scores. Or at least, got mine to within one of hers, so I was an idiot and I missed a spectacular opportunity. As the song goes, "what kind of fool am I?"

Abigail. Abigail. Abigail. I wonder what she's doing now? I wonder if she's still got that hat? And I wonder where she got it from?

I had a little fantasy about her a few years ago where I tracked Abigail down and told her I was ready to take up her offer. It was only a fantasy, of course, because I couldn't see how she'd still be up for it some fifteen years on. Not the sort of delayed decisiveness that gets a girl hot under the collar. Still, the fantasy was great. I would be out and about and I'd bump into her in the shops and we'd pick up from where we left off. My heart would be pumping with excitement, the way it had done all those years ago, and after a while, Abigail would lean close, smile and give me that unmistakeable look.

"Hmm, still a big boy, I see," she'd whispered, slipping her hand back inside my trousers. "Very big indeed. Now how about that fuck? Do me good and hard!"

The fantasy would then head off to the toilet, or a motel, or a car park, or the woods, or anywhere else I'd decide to take it and we'd indulge in fantastically frantic sex, the sort of sex in fact I'd not known for a long long time. And that would be that.

Occasionally I'd grind a little fact into the fantasy.

I'd think about looking her up on friendsreunited.com and work out in my mind how I'd approach her, what I'd say and where we'd meet and all the rest of it and that factual foundation would make the fantasy even more exciting.

Of course, I'd never really do it. Not in a million years. Abigail was gone, or at least part of a different time line now, and I was here all on my own still screwing my face up and holding my head in my hands every time I thought about the incident fifteen years on.

"Sandwiches!" a voice called from around the corner.

Tom leapt up from his seat and bolted in the direction of the corridor, dodging in front of two secretaries and his designer as he raced for first pick.

"Do you want anything?" Elenor smiled, standing on her tiptoes in order to lean across the partition and look down at me.

I hadn't earlier. But suddenly I wasn't so sure.

Sally's Diary: January 11th

OUR HAMSTER died at school today. I don't know why, she wasn't very old, and none of the kids had been using her for batting practice, so it's something of a mystery. Her name was Samantha and she was eight months old. I mention these things purely for posterity as it makes me sad to think of something that inspired so much love and happiness in so many children being forgotten about the moment she's gone. We haven't actually told the children yet and there's some division as to how we should go about it. Jenny thinks we should do tomorrow's assembly on hamster heaven and how fantastic it is up there, while Donald thinks we should tell them Samantha's cage is being redecorated while we order another. Peter thinks we should stick the cage on eBay and split the money but Carol's got most experience with this sort of thing. She says we should just tell the children that Samantha died and let them learn to deal with it. After all, death is a part of life and it's our job to prepare them for what lies ahead, so sugar coating every little upset isn't going to help them in the long run. She has a point. That's the thing about Carol. She always has a point.

Andrew, on the other hand, rarely seems to have one. He's convinced Samantha was murdered and thinks we should set up an investigation into her "hamstercide". He even offered to come in and head up the inquiry, promising to leave no stone unturned until he found Samantha's killer, although he hardly inspired me with confidence when I mentioned her to him again half an hour later and he asked me who Samantha was.

CHAPTER 8.
PARTY GAMES

MY ROOM WAS on the sixth floor and afforded me a great view of Croydon – if that can be considered a great view. Norman had negotiated a discount rate for all of us who wanted to stay but my single was still costing me £80. A twin or double would've cost only £20 more and Tom hassled me all week to share with him but I insisted on having my own room.

"Why? What d'you need your own room for? It's not like I haven't seen you in your socks before."

"I'd just rather have my own room, that's all. We're not students any more, I don't want to doss down any old place."

"Sharing a room in a four-star hotel and saving us both thirty quid in the process is hardly dossing down any old place. What are you up to?"

"I'm not up to anything."

"Then why won't you share with me?"

"Because I don't want to."

"Are you getting your room for free or something? Is that it?" This conversation went on all week and almost threatened the return of my tenner but Tom eventually relented when he found himself a B&B half a mile down the road for only £40.

"Should've blagged a few caravans and we could've all kipped in the car park," Godfrey reckoned.

"I'm sure the Croydon Park Hotel would've loved that," I replied.

Anyway, back to my room. It was nice and roomy and soft and plush. It was also only a short lift journey away from our party downstairs (Joe Bananas having been already booked). I checked in at six, showered, shaved and changed into my party frock, then cracked open a bottle of Jim Beam I'd bought from the off-licence around the corner and took a couple of sneaky knocks. I hoped the hotel wouldn't mind but I bought it in case I wanted a nightcap when the party wound down and mini-bars were always so expensive. And the drinks showed up on your bills too. And bills were sometimes looked at by others. And that might not be such a good thing. Especially if someone else wanted to come up to my room for a nightcap.

At that moment my mobile rang and I saw it was Sally. I pressed the green button and held it to my ear.

"Hello love, just me," she said. "Just giving you a quick ring to see if you want me to record *Taggart* tonight?"

"Oh, er yes please," I replied, a little off-guard. "Thanks."

It was the last part of a three-part story tonight and there's no point watching the first two episodes unless you're ready to commit to all three. Stupid symbolic irony.

"Enjoy the party then and don't get too drunk."

"I won't. What are you doing?"

"Oh nothing, just a bit of tidying and reading I suppose. I might watch *Big Brother* later if there's nothing else on. Anyway, have fun. Bye love."

"Yes, bye love. See you tomorrow."

I listened until the line went dead then put the phone down and turned it off for the night.

*

The party downstairs was already a feeding frenzy of arms and elbows as five thousand years of civilisation was forgotten in the face of a free bar. A couple of streaky barmen rushed backwards and forwards under the taps as they tried to keep pace but the beast was loose tonight and he was thirsty.

"Andrew, you want one?" Tom called from the front of the melee.

"Bitter," I replied fours times before he finally caught it.

A pint was passed back towards me but got lost in the crowd so I had to call for another one to be dispatched. After another ten minutes me, Tom and two pints of John Smiths finally met up and went in search of a table somewhere quieter.

Most years, the Christmas party had been a sit down affair but no one really felt like sitting down to a plate of turkey and sprouts in paper hats in the middle of January, so a buffet had been laid on instead.

"You should try some of those chicken legs, they're lovely. I've had four already," Tom told me.

"Well done," I replied. I took a few sips from my pint and looked around the hall. There was still an enormous knot of blokes fighting over the free bar and the buffet was being continually raided by swooping secretaries but most of the rest of the hall was empty.

Naturally there were a few party martyrs dotted about here and there and some DJ off in the far corner playing with himself but the party was still several hours of hard drinking away from anything approaching fun.

"Who are you looking for?" asked Tom, after he spotted me scouring the darkness.

"No one."

"Really? Well you look like a man who's looking for someone."

That wasn't good. I didn't want to look like a man who was looking for someone because people might start to notice and wonder who that particular man was looking for. And why.

"Just seeing who's in," I thought to elaborate. Tom left it at that.

"By crikey, this is going down well," he gasped dramatically, wiping his mouth with the back of his hand and finishing his pint at a canter. He stared at me for several seconds, as I took a gentle sip of my half-full pint, before finding the need to shake his glass in my face.

"Come on, it's your round," he told me.

"It's a free bar Tom," I pointed out.

"Yeah, but I went up and got the last one. Now it's your turn."

"Get it yourself," I told him, damned if I was going anywhere near that scrum while I still had a drink.

Tom kicked the table and sighed, muttered and growled as I nursed my pint for as long as I possibly could, but he was equally damned if he was going up again and snapped at me to "fucking drink up" every time I tried to engage him in conversation. When I finally drained the last few suds Tom practically tipped me out of my seat and told me to get four pints and a couple of shorts while I was up there.

"Give us a shout when you're getting served and I'll come up and grab them off you."

That didn't look like any time soon as most of the rest of the company had the same idea and were ordering as much as they could before the bar started charging.

Off to one side, the wankers from *Xtreme Kite Surfing Magazine* had formed a chain and were attempting to bury a table at the back of the hall in pints, pissing everyone else off something rotten. They'd monopolised one of the barmen for more than fifteen minutes, leaving just one other lad to serve the rest of the company and tempers were starting to fray. One or two blokes attempted to steal pints from the *Xtremers*' (as they insisted on calling themselves) larder but a couple of them stayed back to protect it and the whole thing threatened to kick off.

Incredibly, it didn't occur to them, or more likely, they just didn't care that the reason the bar was so congested was because of their hoarding and they would've continued all night had Norman not stepped in and suggested they tried drinking what they had before ordering any more. The *Xtremers* naturally tugged their forelocks the moment Norman took notice but were back boasting and toasting their mischief with their trademark crossed forearm X salutes as soon as he was gone.

They were wankers.

The extra barman told on the waiting time so I was able to make it to the front, attract his attention, lean in some of the *Xtremers*' spilt beer and make it back out again with four pints and two shorts in a little under ten minutes.

"I'll tell you, if that's what it takes to get a couple of free pints, I'd rather pay for my bloody beer," I concluded.

I took heart from the fact that the drinks I'd gathered would probably see us through to the last stampede when the free bar closed. And when that nightmare unfolded, it would be Tom's turn again.

I sat back down and was just about to get tucked into the fruits of my labours when a long pair of legs suddenly appeared next to me.

"Oh hi, you came. I'm so glad you did," Elenor squeaked excitedly.

I turned around, looked her up and down and practically bristled all over when I saw how stunning she looked. She was always sexy, of course, even around the office, but suddenly she'd polished up like half a million quids' worth of sex vouchers. I could scarcely think to speak. Her hair had been piled up on top of her head in some kind of exquisite bun, leaving just a couple of curls to keep her temples company. Her neck was bare and her shoulders naked, a tiny strap kept her gold sequinned top from collapsing under the weight of her enormous tits and she'd managed to find a tight lycra belt that could double as a mini skirt. Her legs were a golden nylon sheen and tan loops that peered from under the hem of her skirt told me she'd worn stockings and suspenders rather than cluttering things up with tights. All these garments and a scattering of silver were piled on top of a pair of pointed stilettos that looked like they could've been used for keyhole surgery and which added three inches to her height while taking away half a stone in weight.

She was, for want of a better expression, a shag just waiting to happen.

"Yes," I finally replied, figuring I should say something before I tossed my marriage certificate over my shoulder and leapt on top of her.

She twisted her legs and chewed on her lip for a bit before feeding me my line.

"So, do you want to get me a drink?"

"Yes, sure," I said automatically before remembering what that entailed. "Oh bollocks."

Tom looked at me from the safety of his pint and told me to get us both another couple of shorts in if I was going up and suddenly I was in the thick of it again, fighting my way through bedlam while Elenor's cheeks warmed my seat.

"'scuse me. Sorry. Coming through. Can I just... Sorry!"

I spent the best part of fifteen minutes chanting things

like these and slicing my way through the tangled nest of bodies before I made it back out to daylight with two gin & tonics and two more whisky singles.

"Wasn't there any ice?" Tom asked when I handed him his.

"Oh piss off," I snapped back.

"Cheers," I told Elenor, tipping my glass against hers.

"Bottoms up," she replied with a wink, causing me to shiver right through to my vows as I pictured her bottom bent over my hotel bed.

My God, was this really happening? Surely not? Surely… I stifled my shiver with a shot of warm scotch and sent two gulps of bitter after it to chase it through my system.

"So, will you be dancing later?" Elenor asked.

Tom rasped his lips in derision and looked to me to do the same but I turned his world upside down when I told her, "sure, I might have a dance later on. After a few more drinks, of course."

Tom furrowed his brow in my direction and touched the start-up button in his brain. He'd been hoping not to have to use it tonight but suddenly something was afoot. He was cautious enough not to lend his questions a voice, but he did start taking notes.

I wondered if I should tip Elenor the wink to be careful around Tom, but then I remembered that we'd never actually come to any proper sort of understanding and I was somewhat reluctant to go wandering into uncharted territories without a nod of approval.

I decided the best way forward was fog, so I told Tom not to be such a misery guts and join us for a dance. Surprisingly, Elenor didn't jump in to object. In fact, she even agreed and told Tom she wanted to see him shaking his stuff before the night was out, and I took a moment to fret over what this all meant.

I finally got it boiled down to six possibilities:
Elenor was playing along and being circumspect.
Elenor fancied Tom.
Elenor wanted to play us off against each other.
Elenor wasn't bothered which of us she got.
Elenor wanted both of us – at the same time.
Elenor wanted neither of us and this was all in my head.

The last of these possibilities was possibly the most probable, but by that same token there had been a dramatic shift in Elenor's behaviour towards me over the last month, of that there was no denying. I'm not an expert in these things, of course, all I could go by was my own experiences, but they were telling me she was definitely interested.

How did I know this?

By the way she looked at me. And I'd seen this look before, some fifteen years earlier, beneath the brim of a hat, in a dark and dingy Student Union bar.

"I like your suit, where did you get it?" Elenor asked, sliding her fingers into my jacket to feel my lapel.

"Nowhere expensive," I admitted, and wondered if she'd let me do the same to her top. I concluded she would.

"Look at those wankers over there," Tom hissed, staring at the Xtremers like a sniper who's rifle was at the menders. "They're doing it again."

Me and Elenor looked over and sure enough the Xtremers were restocking their table after barely touching their cache.

"I'm going to say something because this isn't on," Tom declared, rising from his seat and taking a few determined strides towards their table.

"Come on Andrew, are you coming or what?" Tom asked.

Elenor's eyes flickered across my line of sight and a faint

smile glanced her lips when I told Tom I was fine where I was. Tom continued to stare at me before asking if he could have a quiet word "in private like".

A guilty cloud quickly engulfed me but I was able to climb out from beneath it and shape my face into an innocent gawp before we found ourselves alone.

"What's up?" I asked.

"You tell me pal. What are you up to with her?"

"Who?" I attempted.

"Don't give me that. Her. Elenor. Who d'you think I'm talking about?"

I built up my most convincing gasp of indignation then slammed on the brakes and toned it down at the last moment when I decided I shouldn't know what he was talking about right away.

"What d'you mean?"

"You know exactly what I mean, mush."

"What?" I let that hang for a moment, then did a silver-screen double-take and demanded to know just what Tom was implying.

"Don't give me that, you just listen to me; don't be a fucking idiot."

"I don't know where you've..."

"I don't care," Tom slapped me. Yes, he actually slapped me, albeit a very quick, light cuff around the chops. "You just don't be a fucking idiot, and I mean it."

"Hang on a minute..."

"No, I haven't got a minute. I'm sorry if I'm wrong, and I really hope I am, but you'd better pull your head out of your arse and think about what you're doing, because this could be without doubt the stupidest thing you've ever done in your entire fucking life," he said, then added as an afterthought,

"And that's saying something."

"Tom, you've got this all wrong…"

"Good, I'm glad. I'm really really glad I've got it wrong. Just you make sure it stays that way," he concluded, then headed off to chin a couple of Xtremers while staring back at me over his shoulder.

"What was all that about?" Elenor asked.

Tom's words had followed me back to my seat like a bad smell and they got stinkier the moment Elenor smiled up at me. I debated what to tell her and plumped for a spun and slanted version of the truth.

"Oh, it's just silly really," I faffed. "He thinks there's something going on between us."

"Like what?" she asked, shifting in her seat and twisting her legs around each other like a couple of pipe cleaners.

"You know," I prompted.

"No what?" she maintained.

"You know!" I shrugged, nodded and flapped my eyebrows but Elenor still refused to fill in the blanks.

"What?" she insisted.

I took a deep breath and an even deeper swig of my pint then told her, "He thinks we're… well… you know, sleeping together."

Elenor threw back her head and laughed – a little too heartily for my liking – and said she thought that was hilarious.

"Honestly, how people talk," she said, shaking her head and smiling out of the side of her face. She then leaned forward and said very huskily, "Well, we'll have to be careful then, won't we?"

Sally's Diary: January 13th

WHILE THE cat's away, the mice will play. But then those mice probably had other mice they could phone up at short notice and play with. My mice are all busy with their rats. This is one of the fundamental drawbacks about being part of a couple – you can't seem to do anything on your own anymore.

I called my friend Alison to see if she was doing anything and she told me she was going out with her husband for dinner. She qualified this by inviting me and Andrew along but Andrew's at his January Christmas party and I'd feel funny about sitting down to dinner with another couple if it was just me by myself.

Debbie is equally tied up with her bloke and Sophie's tiling the kitchen (on a Friday night? Sounds like an excuse to me) and that's just about all my friends. Funny, I thought I had more than that.

I guess most of my friends now reside beyond that two-year barrier which always adds weirdness to out of the blue calls so maybe I'll get a DVD instead.

I hope Andrew doesn't get too drunk tonight. I always fear for him when he is, particularly when he's in the same room as Norman. He can be so impulsive at times although I know it's not really him. Andrew's a sweet man, who's just given over to acts of foolishness, often fuelled by alcohol.

I just know he's going to come home tomorrow morning kicking himself about something. I just hope it isn't anything he can't take back.

CHAPTER 9.
LATER THAT SAME EVENING

I DIDN'T KNOW if Elenor had been joking or serious or flirting or what when she'd said we'd have to be careful. All I knew was everything about infidelity was infuriatingly vague. So vague in fact that even I didn't know if there was any infidelity going on between me and Elenor. But then I guess that's the nature of the beast.

We talked for another ten minutes or so but none of it went anywhere near anything too risqué and before it had a chance to we were suddenly inundated on all sides by work colleagues in paper hats.

A few of the more boring secretaries tried to entertain us with their old lady ventriloquist acts, which consisted of them talking non-stop while jamming a foot-wide slice of cake into their faces, so Elenor took the opportunity to slip away into the shadows.

I managed my escape a few minutes later, under the false flag of going to get some more food, and the whole table started handing me their plates.

"Here, bring me back a couple of those prawn things and some mini-sausages, would you? And some bread and a bit more cake," one particularly repugnant and deluded eating machine called Rosemary instructed me. Rosemary was fifty-eight years old and a tediously proud grandmother of three who considered herself the matriarch of the company. In practical terms this meant she thought she could boss, nag and order everyone else about on account of her age even though she was only a secretary – and a fucking dreadful one at that.

Her plate went straight in the bin.

I spent the next hour circling the hall in an attempt to get near Elenor again without making it too obvious. I didn't want to follow her around all evening like some love-struck teenager, but at the same time I didn't want to play it so cool that I missed my opportunity – if there even was an opportunity to be missed.

The other thing I had to consider was Tom. Fresh from his triumph of confronting the *Xtremers* and calling them "a big bunch of gays with kites", he was now shadowing me like Philip Marlowe on time and a half. It was getting a little wearing to be honest. Every time I looked around he was a dozen yards away leaning against a pillar or post and boring his eyes into me. Once or twice he'd give me a wink, but most of the time he'd just stare.

The bloody hypocrite, I thought to myself when I came out of the men's room and almost walked straight into him. How many women had Tom boasted he'd shagged in the past? Half of them were married too, well not half, but a fair few and he'd just shrugged his shoulders and told me he could only screw what he could only screw.

Which still didn't make any sense.

I went to the bar, ordered another drink and decided I needed to work on a plan of action otherwise I'd end up with the interfering git camped out at the end of my bed if I wasn't careful.

"Oi, where were you?" a voice said behind me.

"What?" I replied, turning to see an angry Rosemary wagging a finger in my direction.

"Where were you? And where's my plate? I waited for three quarters of an hour waiting for you to come back but you never did. By the time I got up there all those little prawn things had gone and there was hardly anything left! Where were you?" she demanded.

"What am I, your footman or something?" I asked, turning my back on her.

"Why of all the... you should learn a bit of respect, you should. I'm fifty-eight years old, you know and in my day if you was to..."

"Listen Rosemary, I don't want to be rude or anything but... I'm going to be. So sod off."

Rosemary had never been talked to like this before in her life. I know this because she told me so. And I also now know she had two big strapping sons who'd come down here and beat my brains in for daring to talk to her like that, but no amount of tearful phone calls could lure either of them away from the telly, so she had to settle for sobbing in the corner of the hall for twenty minutes and spilling her guts to anyone who would listen, including Norman.

Norman came to see me shortly afterwards to ask if I'd be willing to apologise, so I asked him what for. "She said you said something dreadful to her, something too terrible to repeat," he tutted sadly.

"No, not really. I just told her to sod off."

This surprised Norman. "Really? Is that all? Oh."

"Why, what did she say I'd said?"

"She didn't, so I just assumed you'd called her a... a... well you know," he said, raising both eyebrows to indicate he was talking worse case scenario here. "Or maybe told her to go and stick something somewhere."

"No, just sod off."

"Oh. Well look, would you apologise to her anyway please, just for the sake of appearances? You don't have to mean it or anything," Norman coaxed.

I sighed heavily and sagged my shoulders. I could see there was no way out of this palaver without one of us making some sort of contrition and seeing as Rosemary was the sort of person who wholeheartedly believed she'd never done anything wrong in all her life, I knew it had to be me. This kind of went back to Tom's "being a man and taking the blame" theory, though at the time I'd assumed this only applied to women you fancied.

Naturally Rosemary accepted my apology with all the good grace of a seven-year-old being told bedtime had been brought forward three hours and did her level best to build the biggest mountain possible out of the materials available until finally even Norman had had enough and we left Rosemary and several other elderly secretaries to it, to strains of, "an apology's not an apology if he doesn't mean it, and he doesn't mean it… whahh boo-hoo" etc.

This was triply annoying because it focused all sorts of unwanted attention on me when I wanted to tiptoe through the party unnoticed and manoeuvre myself into pole position with Elenor. There was suddenly fat chance of that now that I had Norman bending my ear, Tom tailing my every move and an assorted dozen secretaries and suits scolding me or slapping me on the back respectively.

"Well, I guess it wouldn't be a party if someone didn't get upset," Norman eventually concluded. "Anyway, how's that lovely wife of yours? Sally? Is she keeping well?"

"Yes, she's fine," I replied.

"You know, I've always liked her, on the occasions that I've met her. Charming lady, Andrew. You've got a real good one there," he congratulated. "What's she up to these days?" he then asked.

"Oh, you know, same old same old," I frowned, a trifle

reluctant to launch chapter and verse into a gushing eulogy about the charming lady I was considering doing the dirty on.

"Is she still teaching, at all?"

Christ Norman, here's her number. Just go and phone her and ask her yourself, was what I felt like saying but in the event I just mumbled something about classrooms and kids and such like then told him I had to go to the loo.

"I'll get you another pint in for when you come back," Norman said, completely taking it for granted I was coming back. This just served to annoy me further, because I hadn't even really needed the loo, I was just trying to put a page break between me and Norman and shake off one set of meat hooks. Now I was going to be stuck with him for at least another twenty minutes and possibly longer if he started to look like he'd quite like a pint back.

In which time anything could've happened to my plans.

"I might just have a short," it suddenly occurred to me.

"Yeah, that's not a bad idea."

"Scotch straight up."

"Make that two, and make them doubles," Norman told the barman, then he stopped me in my tracks when he added, "And get us a couple of pints too."

I decided to go to the loo anyway, just to regroup my thoughts, though I was stopped three times on the way there by different people all wanting to know what I'd done to upset Rosemary.

"Did you really call her a 'fat boring old bitch?" Roger from accounts asked – a blend of Chinese whispers and Rosemary's popularity at work there no doubt.

When I finally shook off the last of my admirers I walked out into the hotel reception and almost fell over myself when I saw Elenor and Godfrey near the main stairs. They were talking in hushed tones but I could tell, even from this distance, that whatever it was they were talking about the discussions weren't going well. Godfrey's demeanour was that of a man desperately trying to make a woman understand something, whereas Elenor's body language cried I understand, I just don't care. I backed up a few steps and tried spying on them through the gap in the door when Tom tapped me on the shoulder.

"What are you doing?" he asked.

"Look, why don't you just clear off and stop following me around?" I demanded, pushing him back into the hall before Elenor and Godfrey spotted us.

"Not until you tell me what you're up to," he replied, jabbing his finger into my chest.

"I was going to the toilet, if you must know."

"Funny place to do it. They've got bogs just across reception, you know."

He was about to say something else when one of the *Xtremers* walked past and told me I was a "bad bad boy for talking to a little old lady like that".

"Can everyone just fuck off and leave me alone?" I asked, exacerbated.

"Well manners cost nothing and a woman of that age…" he started but Tom cut him short and told him this was a private conversation and suggested he go and fly his "fucking kite" in some other playground.

"Oh, it's you," the *Xtremer* then realised, taking a step into Tom's face. "You want to go outside or something?"

"After you fun boy," accepted Tom, squaring up to him like the heavyweight *Camper Van Magazine* editor he was.

"Hang on a minute…" I started, but Tom told me it was fine, he could take this "idiot" no problem and backed that statement up with a wink.

"Let's go then," the guy said and started walking towards the main exit, only to stop and turn when he realised neither me nor Tom were following him.

"I told you this is a private conversation, I'll be out in a minute," Tom said.

"I'll be waiting," the *Xtremer* growled, pushing his way manfully through the revolving door.

"Fucking right you will," Tom told me, checking his watch. "Five quid says he's still there in ten minutes."

"Getting back to the point, do you want to enjoy your own party and let me enjoy mine?"

"Depends on who else you're planning on inviting."

"How has what I do got anything to do with you anyway?" I asked.

"Because I'm your mate, I'm looking out for you," he insisted.

"Well why don't you go and look out for me somewhere else and get off my back? I wasn't doing anything anyway, I was just…" I said, but trailed off.

"Just what?"

"Just… I don't know. That's the point, I don't know what I was going to do. Nothing, probably. I just wanted to…"

"Fuck Elenor?" Tom nodded, finishing my sentence for me.

"No!" I denied.

"Feel her tits?"

"Of course not."

"Stick your dick in her gob?"

"Stop it!"

"Look, you can dress it up any old way you want but there's really only one name for it. You want to look at, touch and feel Elenor's rude bits and have her look at, touch and feel yours. That's called sex. Even if she just sucks you off or talks dirty to you over the phone while you're looking at pictures of her in her pants, it's still the wobbly side of fidelity. I mean, if you're only going to do that, you might as well go the whole way and bang her tits off because it all boils down to the same thing in the end."

"Which is?" I asked, realising I was going to hear this lecture one way or another so it was best if I just let him get it off his chest.

"Sally wouldn't like it."

"Sally doesn't like lots of things," I pointed out.

"This isn't you doing the crossword on the bog for half an hour, this is the big one. The no turning back one. The really fucking stupid one. You think about it."

And with that he finally wandered off.

*

If that wasn't enough, when I got back to the bar I suddenly remembered Norman was still there waiting for me with a year's supply of John Smiths.

"Thought you'd fallen in," he joked.

"Oh, for fuck's sake....!" I mumbled to myself as Norman handed me an enormous tumbler full of whisky.

"Ah no, just having to explain to someone else about Rosemary. Is she still milking it?"

"Yes she's got her coat from the cloakroom but she hasn't actually gone anywhere yet. I think she's waiting for someone to ask her not to go before she goes," Norman concluded. That was quite good for Norman so I smiled accordingly and decided I'd better ask him a few questions about Christmas, family and his never-changing wife, just to be polite.

"How's the family?"

"Fine, fine, ever so good. My youngest has just sent off the UCAS forms – you know, for a university place – and is awaiting the results."

"Oh really, Oxford? Cambridge?" I asked.

"Nothing so ambitious, I believe Nottingham's top of the list," he replied.

"Oh yeah, I wonder why?" I laughed, giving him a cheeky dig in the ribs.

"What do you mean?" Norman asked.

"Well, who hasn't heard all the rumours about Nottingham being full of women? Three girls to every boy, apparently. That's half the reason everyone applies to go up there," I said. "Probably the reason your youngest applied."

"Really? I hadn't heard that. I'll have to ask her," Norman said.

At that moment Elenor entered the bar and I was relieved to see that Godfrey was no longer attached to her. She cast me a look as she took her place at the bar next to me then swung her eyes towards Norman and back at me again, all without saying a word.

I felt my mercury rise when I realised that Elenor had been holding my gaze for almost a full five seconds and didn't look like breaking it off any time soon. I went to say something about something but stopped when, unbelievably, out of Norman's line of sight, she aimed a little "shush" at me.

At that moment, I not only knew we were both singing from the same song sheet, I also knew that Elenor was going to suck me off once we'd finished singing.

My heart thumped heavily inside my breast pocket and my trousers tightened divinely around my hips. I twisted my legs at the ankles and adjusted my posture to try and disguise my increasingly obvious excitement but things soon got so bad that I was forced to resort to the old 'hand in the pocket' ploy to cover up the physical evidence of my sinful conclusions.

I don't know if Elenor or Norman noticed, I'm pretty sure they didn't, though there was one set of beady eyes on the other side of the hall that weren't as blinkered.

"Yes it'll be a shame when Anna goes off to university," Norman was saying. "What with Joseph in Leeds and Brian already graduated and living up in Edinburgh, I'm afraid the house is going to seem very empty."

"Yes that happens," I said without really listening.

"And how are you young lady? Enjoying the party?" Norman asked when he finally noticed Elenor standing the other side of me.

"Yes it's fun, a bit like work only with booze and music."

"Are you staying in the hotel tonight?" he then asked.

"I don't know, are you offering?" Elenor replied, momentarily knocking the smile off Norman's face. It soon returned a couple of seconds later with interest and brought with it a big booming laugh that drew a few stares.

"My god, I'm old enough to be your father," he pointed out unnecessarily. "I'm afraid I'll have to respectfully stand aside and leave you to some of the younger chaps."

"Not too young though," Elenor said, shifting her eyes to mine. "I prefer my men to have a modicum of experience."

She took a tantalising little sip of her drink then seeped away from the bar in thirteen heel-to-toe steps before disappearing through the door.

"By crikey someone's going to get it tonight," Norman speculated.

I could no longer speak.

"Anyway, what was I saying? Oh yes, how's that lovely Sally

of yours?" The sound of raised voices and a sudden kerfuffle from across the hall rescued me from this particular question as Norman decided he'd better go and check out what was going on over in the Xtremers' corner.

"... up and... 'sh ... ace in!" I heard someone shout, before a familiar voice questioned the shouter's sexuality and suggested a few places he should "fuck off back to with your fucking windmill".

"Leave it, leave it!"

"Get off of me!"

"I'll fucking have you!"

"Don't Rob, it ain't worth it!"

"Break it up! Break it up!"

Me and Norman pushed our way through to the front just in time to see Tom take an almighty fist in the face. He tried swinging his own fists in defence but he was already motoring back at a full lick and inevitably crashed straight through the *Xtremers'* beer mountain at a hundred miles per hour, arse-first.

I'd never seen fifty pints spilt at one time before and pray I never see it again. A tsunami of lager drowned everyone's feet within a 10 yard radius and the crash of breaking glass caused the DJ to gouge a new verse into *Frosty the Snowman*. A couple of women screamed and I savoured the sight of the other three *Xtremers'* faces as their night's supplies headed for the dance floor before wading in make sure Tom was okay.

Surprisingly, he wasn't too bad. He had a few cuts on his arms, a bit of glass in his hand and his trousers probably wouldn't make it through the night, but other than that he was okay.

Absolutely drenched, but okay.

"You fucking bastard!" he shouted as he held his arms at

right-angles to drain the Stella from his sleeves. "You utter fucking twats!"

"What have you done?" one of the distraught *Xtremers* shouted at his mate.

"It wasn't me it was him. He..."

"Now now, let's all simmer down," Norman interjected. "We're going to need a mop and a bucket," he reckoned, then started ordering people this way and that, breaking off to tell the *Xtremer* who'd thrown the punch that he wanted to see him in his office first thing in the morning, before continuing with the clean up operation.

"Are you all right?" I asked.

"What the fuck do you think?" Tom replied, examining his phone, wallet and fags to find that only one of the three had survived. "Christ al-fucking-mighty!"

I offered him my handkerchief to wipe some of the lager from his eyes and they bore into me with a bloodshot intensity that knew no bounds.

"I'm going to have to go back to my B&B and get changed," he tutted. "Fucking walking half a mile down the road in this weather! The bastard. I'll be back coming back though, don't you worry about that," he warned me before trundling off into the night.

That was it. I didn't have long.

Maybe an hour or so if I was lucky.

I had to speak to Elenor.

CHAPTER 10. CRUNCH TIME

I FOUND ELENOR a few seconds after Tom found the exit. Several people had attempted to detain me with a load of pointless questions about what had happened to Tom (Rosemary – still with her coat on her lap – muttered, "I thought he'd be involved" as I walked past) but I didn't break stride until I found Elenor.

Once again Godfrey had cornered her and once again he was pleading his case, but Elenor's mind was not only made up, she was actively enjoying the anguish she was causing Godfrey. At least that's how it looked from where I was standing. I'd hung back a couple of yards hoping to grab her when Godfrey finally gave it a rest but the moment Elenor spotted me she turned her back on Godfrey, just as he was reaching the crescendo of his humiliation, and strode purposefully over towards me.

"Hi, are you looking for me?" she asked straight out.

"Er… I… you know, sort of…" I muttered by way of a reply, reluctant to answer any sort of direct question with any sort of direct answer. "Sure."

"What's up?" she grinned, swivelling her hips from side to side and playfully toying with one of her loose curls.

I looked past her at Godfrey and saw all the misery and suffering of the world etched onto his face. He made no attempt to disguise his glare and kicked the last few fragments of his own shredded dignity into touch by studying us for signs of intimacy.

"Had a fight?" I asked, nodding towards Godfrey.

"Hmm?" Elenor feigned, then laughed. "Oh no, just little boys being little boys."

Elenor looked back over her shoulder during one particularly acute twist of the hips before redirecting her sparkling eyes at me.

"So what's up?" she asked. "What are we doing?"

My heart leapt at the way she'd phrased that. What were *we* doing? I didn't know, but at least there was finally an acknowledgement that we were doing *something*.

Elenor stared at me and chewed her painted lip. It was almost as if she was urging me to ask the question. I wasn't entirely sure what the question was and I certainly didn't want to go bumbling about in the dark without so much as a beacon to head for, so I stared at her for a moment, chewed my own lip (not half as seductively as Elenor) then asked her how it was going.

"Fine," she smiled back twisting me, Godfrey and her loose auburn curls around and around her little finger.

"Good, erm, what was I going to say?" I muttered, causing Elenor's smile to broaden.

Elenor had a lovely smile, really really sexy. Unfortunately I couldn't look at it because every time I tried I caught Godfrey glaring at us as if we were holding him by a leash.

"Godfrey's really staring," I finally told her.

"Let him, I'm not bothered," Elenor shrugged.

"Yeah but it's a little off-putting," I admitted, so Elenor looked over her shoulder, then back at me.

"Okay, let's go to the bar and… have a little chat?" she said. "I'll even let you buy me another drink if you want."

"Okay," I said so we turned and headed back to the party.

My heart was thumping as I fought the rising tide of apprehension, but I knew it was now or never. So, taking a deep deep breath and summoning up all the courage I could muster and grabbed Elenor by the arm.

"Actually, there is something I wanted to say. I want to say… oh why don't you give it a rest and leave me alone you miserable old cow!"

Elenor turned just in time to see Rosemary spin on her heels and run back into the party with a fresh case of waterworks.

"For fuck's sake, can't everyone leave me alone for five minutes?" I asked, then remembered Elenor. "Look, this is going to keep on happening all night, we might never get another moment to have a chat so…"

"Do you have a room here in the hotel?" Elenor suddenly asked.

My heart exploded into a million different pieces and each of those exploded again. "Yes, room 64," I replied, barely believing where this was going.

"And do you have a mini-bar?"

"Yes, and a bottle of scotch I bought from the off-licence," I admitted.

"Even better. We could have a drink in your room if you liked," Elenor suggested. "Just to get some privacy."

"Okay," I agreed.

"But don't you go trying anything on, you dirty bastard," Elenor warned me with a wry smile. "I know what you guys are like once you get a girl into your room. You think you can just chuck us down on the bed and fuck us at will."

"Oh no, no, nothing like that!" I protested, shocked that she should even think such a thing of me.

"Because I wouldn't want it getting around at work that that was what we'd done," she said.

"Of course not, no, God forbid!"

"Good," Elenor said, before drawing close enough to murmur in my ear, "because if we did do anything like that, then I think we should keep it to ourselves. Don't you?"

How I didn't cum in my pants at that moment is a mystery to me. I was the definition of excitement. In fact, if you look 'excitement' up in the *Oxford English Dictionary* you'll see a picture of me standing in the lobby of the Croydon Park Hotel with a really obvious hard-on and a scantily clad secretary. Oxford English put it there to save any confusion over the interpretation.

"I do," I finally agreed, catching Godfrey's eye once more, though this time it was his turn to look away.

*

We sorted out the mechanics of our tête-à-tête with the fewest words possible. Elenor told me to go up to my room and said she'd follow me up in five.

"Just so no one sees us go up together. You know what these gossips are like. Pour me a drink and I'll be up before you know it."

I had a brief vision of me standing up in my room all night looking out of the window at Tom's Xtremer in the car park but something told me it wouldn't come to that. Elenor would be up. Of that I had no doubt.

I twisted the lid off the bottle of Jim Beam once I got up to my room and took an enormous belt. That soothed my nerves just a little, though it did little to appease my excitement. That really needed attending to and I wrestled over the conundrum of how I should go about things with Elenor as I waited for that knock on the door.

Would Elenor lay it on a plate and drop to her knees the moment she was through the door (God I hoped so) or would she see this as a brilliant opportunity to tease me to delirium? Very likely.

Perhaps there was a clue in what she'd said?

"I know what you guys are like once you get a girl into your room. You think you can just chuck us down on the bed and fuck us at will."

That was probably what she was after. She'd come up here and act all coy, then she'd give me a little taster, possibly talk dirty to me, then snatch it back once I'd fallen for her ploy. In the end, that's what I'd have to do. I'd grab her up in my arms, bundle her onto the bed and jump on top of her.

"Oh my, Andrew, whatever are you doing?" she'd giggle, as I peppered her with kisses.

"Shut up! Just shut up and take it!" I'd reply, pulling down her panties and ripping open my fly.

"Are you going to fuck me Andrew? Are you going to give it to me good and proper?"

"Oh God yes. I'm going to give it to you like you wouldn't believe," I'd say.

I'd sink into her with one smooth thrust and… hang on a minute, did I use a condom? Did I stop half way through and tell her to hold her horses while I rooted around the room, found my overnight bag, ripped open the packet of three I'd bought for the evening and stretched a little rubber hat over my pan handle?

"What are you doing in there? Andrew, where are you?"

"Hold on a sec, I put the first one on backwards, now I can't unroll it. Hang on!"

I'd pull the second one out and tear it in half as I opened the foil then fiddle with the third one and mutter and swear as I flicked myself a few times, before finally managing to roll it down my shaft, painfully trapping half a dozen hairs in the process.

"Just coming, almost ready. Sorry about this."

Elenor would still be on the bed, lying in the position I'd left her. Her legs would be open and breasts would be bare.

"What were you doing?"

"Putting on a condom," I'd say, showing her my handiwork.

"Why? This is just a fantasy Andrew. Why are you putting on a condom in your own fucking fantasy?" I didn't get the chance to explain. At that moment there was a knock on the door that made me jump off the bed. My pulse suddenly soared and my stomach was swamped with a million frantic butterflies.

Jesus, she'd come. Elenor had actually come.

In the blink of an eye I saw what lay in store: the seduction, the longing, the having, the passion and the release; the fulfilment of all that I had desired in one insane headlong rush into the unknown and then…

The knock came again.

"Just a moment," I croaked, scurrying up off the bed and folding my eagerness out of sight before making for the door. I was just about to twist the handle when a thought suddenly occurred to me.

What was I doing? What the fuck was I doing?

My hand hovered as my pre-match jitters suddenly mushroomed into an all-out panic attack.

I repeat, what *the fuck* was I doing? I was married. And not just married, I was married to Sally. Oh Jesus, what about Sally? Some might've argued this thought had occurred to me rather late in the day and I would've had trouble disagreeing, but let's put a positive spin on it – at least it *had* occurred to me. Tom's friend Martin, the one who drank in the Duke of York, who'd notched up more than two hundred confirmed conquests; I bet if you asked him for his thoughts on his wife while he was tucking into Miss Two Hundred and One, he'd look up from his perfectly unrolled condom and ask "who?"

Was that who I aspired to be?

Did I really want to be that bastard?

I was a rabbit stuck in the headlights of an oncoming disaster and I didn't have a clue what to do.

If I opened the door, Elenor would come in and I would end up having sex with her. I was sure of that. Oh God, such sweet, intoxicating, fulfilling frantic, insatiable lust – which was everything I desired but probably the worst thing in the world I could do (short of then killing and eating her afterwards).

If, however, I didn't open the door, I'd never get this chance again and I would never ever know the heady exhilaration of illicit ravenous sex ever again – which admittedly would be in keeping with that vow I'd made in front of all those people all those years ago, but which would chew my guts up for the rest of my life.

Just as my Abigail non-adventure did.

What a dilemma!

No matter what I did, I suddenly realised I'd be hanging my head in shame and beating myself up about it tomorrow. It was a lose-lose situation. In fact, it was probably the most lose-loseiest situation I'd ever known and, coming from a perennial loser like me, this was really saying something.

Knock knock knock?

My eagerness flexed in my trousers and pleaded with me to open the door but when I grabbed the handle, my wedding ring clinked against the steel to fire one last warning shot across my bows.

Oh Jesus. Sally…

"Andrew?"

Uh?

"Andrew, are you in there?"

Hang on a minute, that didn't sound like Elenor. Elenor had a sweet, sexy, pouting voice. This voice was pompous, idiotic, annoying and the bane of my working life. I twisted the handle and swept open the door to come face to face with a walking bucket of cold water.

"Ah, you are in. I thought so," Norman said. "Can I come in for a moment?"

I stared at him in open-mouthed confusion before stepping aside to let him in, though the moment I did, I suddenly remembered Elenor. She would be knocking on my door any second now too. Norman would see her. She'd see Norman. What would I say? More to the point, what would they say?

NORMAN: *"What's going on here? Why is she coming up to your room?"*

ELENOR: *"What's he doing here? Is this some sort of set up or something?"*

NORMAN: *"Are you two going to have sex?"*

ELENOR: *"Did you bring him up here to go twos on me?"*

NORMAN: *"Are you asking him or offering it?"*

ELENOR: *"Why, are you interested?"*

NORMAN: *"Are you alright with that?"*

ELENOR: *"Are you?"*

"What?"

"I said are you all right, Andrew? You look a little peaky," Norman asked.

"What? Oh yes, just a little hot and tired from the party. Thought I'd come upstairs for a quick five minute breather," I replied, staring at my door in dismay as I hyperventilated over the impending shitstorm. "I'm fine now so let's go back downstairs. Okay?"

"Actually, there's something I'm afraid I need to tell you."

Norman had a reticence in his voice that pulled my eyes away from the door. He avoided my gaze when I looked at him and frowned as he struggled to find the words.

Boy, did I not like the look of this. What the hell was he about to tell me?

"Elenor's made a complaint and I'm afraid I'm going to have to fire you."

"Elenor's made a complaint and I've had to phone Sally."

"Elenor's made a complaint and it turns out she's actually only twelve."

"Elenor's made a complaint, but more to the point, I'm gay and you have to bang me instead or I'll tell Sally."

"Elenor's made a complaint but none of this matters now that the world is being attacked by flying saucers. Also, I'm gay and you're going to have to... etc"

Or most horrifyingly of all.

"Elenor's not made a complaint and she reckons you still haven't done your report yet."

When Norman didn't speak I realised I was going to have to beat it out of him. "What is it, Norman? Bad news?"

"I'm afraid so," he replied, tightening my screws all over. "I'm afraid it's Tom…"

"What?" I blinked in total confusion. "Hang on, what?"

"I don't know how it happened but the police are here and they say he's been in an accident. He's been run over."

"Run over?" Before this had a chance to sink in, there was another, gentler knock at the door and I yanked it open without thinking to see Elenor leaning against the door frame seductively.

"It's okay, I've already told him," Norman told her, stepping into view and knocking Elenor for six as she went back on her heels. "Oh dear."

I rushed to her assistance and whispered in her ear to keep quiet as I put my arms around her slender young waist and picked her up again.

"Norman's just told me about it, about Tom being run over," I told her, for the benefit of the audience. Elenor's eyes widened but I pinched my face and shook my head until she got the play.

"Ah, yes, you've told him then, have you?" she agreed. "Right. Good."

"Yes, well look, the ambulance has taken him to Mayday Hospital so I'd better go along and see that he's taken care of. I didn't know whether or not you'd want to come along too, seeing as he was… erm, sorry I mean, *is* a friend of yours. I'm going up there now. Andrew?"

I could barely take in what Norman was saying. It was all so unbelievable. Tom had been run over. The ambulance had taken him to hospital. The police were downstairs.

And Elenor had come to my room.

She looked at me long and hard and I looked right back at her. Her dress and her hair and make-up and legs still looked as stunning as they'd looked that first moment I'd laid eyes on them. Only now they were standing in my room.

I soaked her all in but I knew I was just dithering. I had a decision to make and Norman and Elenor were waiting for me to make it.

Sally's Diary: January 14th

SOMETHING TERRIBLE has happened. Tom was run over last night after the Christmas party and the doctor's say he might've broke his back. He's already had one operation just to stabilise him but he's going to need a great many others. They say he might never walk again, which is just awful awful awful. Andrew's taken it really badly and even seems to be blaming himself, but he won't say how or why. I've tried talking to him about why he thinks he's responsible but he won't be drawn on it and we even ended up having a blazing row. I don't know what happened last night but something was clearly said or done and I think I know what it was.

I've always been worried that my time with Tom might surface one day and cause problems for us and that seems to have finally happened. I only hope Andrew and Tom can patch things up between them because Tom's going to need all the friends he can get right now. Poor silly Tom. Whatever else that might've gone on between us, I hope and pray he's going to be okay.

CHAPTER 11.
CLOSE CALLS AND HEALTH WARNINGS

I DID SOMETHING the night of the party I'm not proud of and that Sally can never find out about.

I smoked a whole packet of cigarettes in less than six hours.

Unbelievable. That's like a fag every eighteen minutes. Pretty good going but my lungs felt like they'd been in a fight with a cheese grater the next morning. Holy smoke!

I don't know what came over me. I guess it was a combination of stresses. Stress at skirting so close to infidelity. Stress at Tom's suspicions. Stress at the palaver with Rosemary. Stress at broken backs. And stress at having to sit in a hospital waiting room with only Norman and stress for company. I challenge anyone not to chain smoke twenty fags in those circumstances.

Of course, I couldn't smoke in the hospital so I had an excuse to get away from Norman and go and wear circles in the car park, and it was out there, in that bitter January darkness that I did some serious thinking.

My thoughts came in no particular order, they were all jumbled up and piled on top of each other, with no single thought taking centre stage over the rest of the pile but one of the more recurring images was of Elenor standing in my room and urging me with her eyes to stay.

Unfortunately I couldn't. Or should that be fortunately? I don't know.

Under laboratory conditions, with soft lights and candles, music and privacy and a signed and sealed permission slip from Sally I would've undoubtedly sucked Elenor from her dress and written off the hotel bed. But I didn't. Because my friend in hospital, my boss at the door, a taxi ticking over downstairs and Sally – my wife Sally – was waiting for me at home. And whatever else I chose to do, the next morning I would have to drive back to Camberley, park the car, take a deep breath and try to pick up everything from where I'd left it the previous day.

And I couldn't have done that had I spent the night with Elenor.

I know some people can – Tom's mate Martin, who drank in the Duke of York, being the obvious case in point – but I simply wouldn't have been able to. I mean, if you think about it, what a terrible burden to shoulder. And not just for a day or a week or a year, but for the rest of my life, because unless I split from Sally, I could never have told her, not unless I wanted to prompt said split. And even then I still couldn't because it would've devastated her. Married, divorced, estranged or even forgotten; it didn't matter because who wanted to know that their loved one had cheated on them while they were together? If we lived to be a hundred and never had another argument again I still wouldn't be able to tell her. Not because of what I feared the consequences might be (although there was that too) but because it would make her unhappy.

And all of a sudden, all I could see was Sally's unhappiness.

Elenor's legs, her bum, her provocative lip-chewing and her curls had all but disappeared from my thoughts so that all I could see was Sally huddled over in her hands, bawling with despair and asking me over and over again why I'd done it.

It sent a shiver done my spine just thinking about it and that shiver started dancing with a shudder when I realised how close I'd come.

Cue another fag.

What really amazed me though was just how quickly my mind had snapped shut. Only a few hours earlier I'd been following Elenor around and whispering conspiratorially in her ear. One calamity later and I was suddenly back to DefCon 5 and dumbfounded at how I could've let things escalate beyond fantasy so spectacularly. Because it would've happened, wouldn't it? It had moved up to the next level and was no longer a game, or a daydream or a flirtatious little misunderstanding.

It would've been an affair.

I had almost had an affair.

Me?

Unbelievable.

Tom had been dead right about everything, which made an astonishing change. He'd known and had tried to steer me away from danger even when I'd been determined to blunder into it three sheets to the wind. He'd tried to protect me and had done so by taking on my arch-nemesis – namely, my own stupidity.

He'd done that for me?

Incredible. You think you know someone, you think they're a bit of a dickhead, then out of the blue they go and do something like that for you.

Wasn't life a rollercoaster?

And wasn't Tom a friend? A true friend.

Well, I'd not let him down again. I'd see to it that I never did anything to disappoint him again and repay him with the sort of friendship he'd shown me. Starting right now. Because right now was when Tom needed me most and I'd ensure he never had to go looking again.

"How is he, sister?" I asked the nurse, when me and Norman arrived at the hospital.

"Who?"

"Tom Castelli. You brought him in probably half an hour ago. He'd been run over," we had to explain when she didn't immediately know off the top of her head who we were talking about.

"Are you his family?"

"No, we're colleagues. We were at the party with him."

"I see," she glared. I didn't know what it was she thought she saw but I suspect it was me and Norman pouring booze down Tom's throat and shoving him in front of the traffic.

We had to wait for another three hours until his brother arrived before we got someone on the inside and thankfully things weren't anywhere near as bad as we'd first feared.

"He's broken his left arm, his left leg and his hip, and he's cracked a few ribs and lost both of his front teeth."

"Thank God for that," Norman had honestly said. Yeah, what a result!

Still, that little insurance windfall was a million times better than a broken back, which was what Norman had first reckoned, filling my head with images of quadriplegics, breathing apparatus and life support system being accidentally unplugged by headphone-wearing Costa Rican janitors.

I don't even know where Norman had got Tom's broken back diagnosis from and asked him why he'd told me that. Norman said the police or the hotel porter or a barman had told him "or something like that," earning himself a matronesque telling off from a nearby nurse for propagating "unnecessary scare stories".

"I'm very sorry sister. Sorry Andrew. I'm... just... ... sorry."

Norman was embarrassed and after my initial anger had subsided I actually felt for him. After all I had already phoned Sally and told her the same so I'd been just as irresponsible, hadn't I?

Anyway, the relief over the news of Tom's true condition was tempered by the reality that he'd still done a pretty decent job on himself, broken back or not, and that he was going to need weeks, if not months, of care and rehabilitation.

"I'll be there for him," I promised his brother. "I don't care what it takes, I'll see that Tom will walk again, even if I have to convalesce him myself."

Fortunately, the hospital said they had nothing else on at the moment so they'd do it if I wanted, letting me off the hook somewhat and setting Tom's brother's mind at ease, though I still promised to do my bit.

"Anything he needs, anything at all and he's got it," I reassured him.

I figured it would be a long, gruelling and doubtlessly painful process getting him back on his feet. A broken leg and a broken hip? Plus a broken arm, so that he couldn't even support himself on crutches. Tom was going to have to use a wheelchair and there was no getting around that. Mobility would be a problem for him so I'd be Tom's legs for the next few weeks. If he needed shopping, pushing around the park, taking to the pub, or just a bit of good old-fashioned company, I'd be the thorn in his side.

"Swimming," Norman had said. "They say that's very good for recovery. Gets the muscles working without putting a strain on the bones."

Then that was it. I'd take Tom swimming every morning for as long as it took him to walk again. I didn't care if it meant going around his flat and dragging him out of his malaise, I'd do this for Tom just as he'd done what he'd done for me (mentioning no specifics). I'd be his best friend and most gruelling taskmaster. I'd get his legs stronger than ever and be there for him when he took his first tentative steps. I'd support him every inch of the way and Tom would hate me for the relentless bastard I'd become, but eventually I'd coax a few steps out of him and once I had those, I'd get some more.

We'd stand together, walk together and eventually run together again.

They say it sometimes takes a disaster to unlock your true potential and this would undoubtedly be the case with Tom. And with me, come to that.

If I could just get him running, who knows what we could achieve together.

Walks for peace?

Coast to coast?

Ben Nevis?

Or most testing of all, the London Marathon? What an accomplishment that would be! From virtual cripple to marathon runner in a single year. It would be like one of those stories of hope and courage that they featured on the news. Like Michael Watson or half the cancer wards in Britain; they all empty out come Marathon time and every one of those brave, courageous heroes was an inspiration to others. Tom could be an inspiration.

No, *we* could be an inspiration.

From death's door to marathon winners… all right, maybe that was taking it a bit too far. From death's door to marathon *heroes*.

Tom and Andrew, best friends and icons of hope for a new generation.

Sally's Diary: February 7th

I'M RELIEVED to see there doesn't seem to be any lasting animosity between Andrew and Tom. I guess they must've talked it through when Andrew went up to visit him last week because they seem to be getting on together again now that Tom's been released, though Andrew can still be a little testy from time to time. Only this evening, Tom phoned for a chat and Andrew refused to speak to him complaining that he was "having his dinner!" Still, he has done lots for him these last few weeks what with all the shopping, visits and errands. Tom was particularly taken by the rails Andrew fitted to the toilet wall in his flat but when his landlord went round and saw them last night he said the cracked tiles would come out of Tom's deposit. Some people are just rubbish, aren't they? Anyway, the two of them are getting on well, which is good, though I'm not sure Tom's particularly keen on running any marathons with Andrew, which is just as well because there's as much chance of Andrew running in the London Marathon as there is of me fitting into a size 12 dress seven months from now.

That's right dear diary, Andrew's no longer the only one eating for two. I am with child. And I can't stop smiling about it. I've heard enough people say you should never tell anyone until you've had the twelve week scan, to make sure, God willing that everything is okay but I guess it's only fair I let Andrew in on it. After all, he's the one that's going to have to get up in the middle of the night to change the baby's nappy. Oh yes he can forget about Ben Nevis, the London Marathon and all the charity treks he likes, but there's one set of rashly-made promises he made a few years back that he's going to be held to.

CHAPTER 12.
SNICKERS MAN

"OH, FOR FUCK's sake, because I don't want to. You go and run a fucking marathon if it's that easy, I'll watch you on telly."

"Tom, that's hardly the spirit that made this country great. You have to rise to the challenge, seize the day and all that. Look at Douglas Bader and what he did. Running a marathon doesn't even compare."

"Yeah well, for your information Douglas Bader flew planes before he had both his legs blown off. He didn't take it up as a hobby afterwards so why should I take up running?"

"You get a medal at the end of the race."

"Yeah well, I could get one on eBay for ten quid if I wanted one that badly. Wouldn't have to run twenty-six miles to get it either. Tenner in an envelope and thank you very much. That'll look lovely on the bog wall next to my OBE."

"There's just no use talking to you," I dismissed, "you'll never get it."

"Get what?"

"Get what it's all about."

"Get what what's all about?" Tom said, then thought about it."

"The point of life," I informed him.

"There's a point? No one told me. So what is it?"

"To make your mark, to make a difference."

"Believe me, me running around London in the back end of a panto horse with you ain't going to make a stroke of difference to no one, least of all Douglas Bader, so we can kick that plan into touch can we?"

"Whatever," I grumbled, annoyed at how he hadn't even thought about it before dismissing it so easily.

"Anyway, what do you want to go running around all over the place for when you've got a kid on the way. You want to go running around after anyone, you should go running around after Sally. How far's she up the stick?"

"A couple of months," I told him, opening one of the bitters I'd brought with me and pouring it into a glass.

"I didn't even know you were trying for a baby?"

"Funny that, neither did I," I replied. "It had been mentioned a few times over the last few years but we'd never actually agreed on anything. Sally said she wanted to try this year but then it just happened naturally. An accident. Oopps, look out mate, you've just made a little person."

"Come off the pill then did she?" he asked, leaning forward out of his wheelchair and reaching for the pack of beers. I passed him a can and he cracked it open and poured it into his own glass.

"No, I don't think so. She says she might've missed a few days here and there over Christmas when she had a bit of a dodgy belly but nothing you could really call deliberate."

"Think it's yours?"

"What sort of a question is that?"

Tom took a big swig of beer to leave himself a fluffy moustache and just shrugged.

"Of course it's mine, whose else is it going to be?"

After a thought Tom suggested his mate Martin, who drank down the Duke of York.

"You never know. Sally's only flesh and zips like the rest of us. And who's to say Sally hasn't been keeping her hand in while you've been gallivanting all over the place after Elenor?"

129

This was fair comment so I let it slide, despite taking exception to the term "gallivanting".

"Sally's not like that," I told him.

"We're all like that," he replied. "And it's always the quiet ones you should always watch out for."

"Sally's anything but quiet. If only. Anyway, what's it to you? Worried it might be yours?" I asked, turning defence into attack.

"Mine? Where d'you get those cards from?"

"Well, you are the only other person I know of that's… you know… been with her, other than me, that is. How do I know you're not knocking her off behind my back?"

"You really are an idiot, aren't you?"

"True, but the point still stands."

"Look, I know you're only joking here, but I just want to say this straight off the bat so that this doesn't all fester in that sick mind of yours and see you coming round here one stormy night to bang on my windows and demand an answer."

Tom took a long sip of beer and lit one of his cigarettes. I almost instinctively asked him if I could have one, but I decided to stay given up for a little while longer. At least until I'd heard what he had to say.

"I am not, and have not, slept with Sally since you got together with her. I had a couple of dates with her back at Uni, as you well know, then she hooked up with you. These days," he said, then shook his head and snorted, "these days Sally wouldn't touch me with a bucket of cold water if I was on fire, so no, unless girls can get it from car seats, I'm pretty confident Sally's baby isn't mine."

"What did go on with you and Sally back at Uni?" I finally asked, catching him unawares. "Come on, it was a long time ago. What's it matter now? So what was it?"

"Has Sally never said anything about it to you then?"

"No, nothing."

"Really?"

"Yeah, really."

"Nothing at all?"

"Tom, she never said anything."

Tom paused to reflect through several deep drags then flicked his ash in the ashtray balanced on the arm of his wheelchair.

"Well I ain't going to say nothing either then," he informed me. "Nothing happened anyway. I don't know what you're on about," he added suspiciously.

"What did you do? Did you… you know?"

"What?" he asked.

"You know?"

"No, what?"

"Look just tell us you bastard!"

Tom stared at me and shook his head.

"If you really want to know, but you're not going to like it," he admitted, angling his eyebrows. He waited the longest possible time before he continued. "We had a foursome," he shrugged, stunning me to my core.

"You mean, like, with another couple?"

"Yeah; Sally, me and another couple of geezers," he nodded. "It was just one of those things, we'd got really drunk and Sally had taken an *e* and it was her idea. She said she wanted to be shagged by three blokes at the same time so she asked the guys next door if they wanted to join in. To be honest, I didn't really enjoy it, I just went along because of her but she wouldn't take no for an answer."

This was considerably worse than I'd been expecting. I

thought it might've been something Tom had done, or failed to do, but Sally and three guys? It was all too much, way too much, but try as I might, there was no putting the cork back in the bottle now.

"She was really going for it you know," Tom winked, all at once miming the incident for me.

"This is a joke. You're joking right?"

"Of course I am you fucking potato-head. What are you like?" I took a moment to mop my brow and dispel the images of Sally "really going for it" with three geezers before draining my glass and asking Tom for a fag.

"No, you've given up," he said, stubbing his cigarette out and slipping his packet into his top pocket. "No, nothing happened between Sally and me. I mean, that was the point, it just wasn't there… for either of us, so we drew a nice little neat line under it and pretended it never happened. Have you been stewing on that for the past… however many years?" he frowned.

"No," I lied.

"Good, because there's nothing to stew on. If anyone should be stewing on anything, it should be me," Tom pointed out.

Tom adjusted his position to demonstrate that the conversation had left him physically uncomfortable then looked down around his wheels for his coat hanger.

"Here it is," I said, spotting it on the floor and handing it to him.

He fed it into his plaster cast and poked about a bit until he found the spot.

"It's going to be great wearing this thing for the next two months," he scratched. "Anyway, what were we talking about? Oh yes, your news. Jesus, you're going to be a dad."

"So you keep saying."

"How do you feel about that?"

"Numb from the eyebrows downwards," I replied.

And I did, more or less. See, Sally's wonderful news came on top of a whole heap of other recent worries and my brain seemed to have responded the way it always did, namely by pretending it hadn't heard. The whole thing simply wouldn't sink in and I couldn't make up my mind how to react, one way or the other. I guess it's often the way with guys. We all say we want kids, just as we all say we want to be in the SAS or the World Cup final, but when it actually happens most of us just freeze, which weeds most of us out of the SAS and World Cup finals, but fatherhood is different.

Anyone can be a father. All that's required is half a bottle of rosé and nothing good on the telly and hey presto, your very own little miracle. How could this not batter a man sideways?

"It's an awesome responsibility," Tom agreed. "So you want it then?"

"What? Of course I want it. Wouldn't you?"

"Yeah I guess, but I'm not the one in the hot seat, am I? Has Sally had the scan and the test and all that now?"

"No, no we've got to do that next week to confirm everything. Actually, I'm not even supposed to tell anyone because they say you're not meant to until you have the scan."

"Why?"

"Well, in case the baby's damaged, or deformed or something and has to… you know, be aborted. It's a bit hard on the mum then having to go back and tell everyone that she's not pregnant any more."

Tom agreed then asked me why I was telling him then.

"Well Christ I've got to tell someone haven't I, I'm going

out of my head. Don't tell anyone else though."

Tom looked around his little empty flat and then down at his plaster casts, wheelchair and silent, dust-covered phone.

"Don't worry, your secret's safe with me."

We talked a little more about Sally and babies and so on, covering all the usual topics such as names, genders and schooling before exhausting all avenues of responsible conversation and got back to the subject of sex.

"So, did you end up giving Elenor one or what?"

"No. I almost did but in the end I didn't," I finally admitted. Tom nodded and said he could see it was heading that way from a mile off. "Yeah well, I don't know what I was thinking," I said. "I wasn't myself."

"Yes you were. Everyone says that when they do something stupid, 'I wasn't myself' but that's bollocks, one up from saying 'it wasn't me, it was some big lads who made me do it'. Sometimes you've got to hold up your hands and take it like a man."

"When did you get so grown up? Only three weeks ago you were replacing Rosemary's granddaughter's picture with a picture of Nick Griffin and blaming it on Godfrey. Now you're holding up your hands and taking it like a man."

"She didn't notice for three days. What a blindo. Anyway, that's different, that was just a joke. What you did doesn't compare."

"Nearly did," I corrected him.

"Fine, nearly did. It still doesn't compare though. You could've fucked up your whole life for the sake of a quick guilty poke. And not just your life, Sally's life too. Did you ever think about that?" he asked.

"Yes yes yes, I thought about it," I assured him, though that sounded even worse so I added, "which is why I didn't go through with it." This wasn't so much a lie, more a fuzzy grey area.

"Well that's for the best," he said. "Believe me, you would've hated yourself for it. Seriously, you would've. Because you love Sally… no no no, I'm not getting soppy or anything, I'm just saying, you do. And if you had ended up banging Elenor you would've felt so guilty that you would've never been able to feel the same about Sally again. And that's a terrible price to pay for a bit of dirty nooky," he lectured.

"Yeah, I know you're right," I said, rubbing my face and reaching for another beer. I passed Tom one too and we paused the conversation to top up our glasses.

"You reckon she is dirty then?" I asked when we resumed. "Old Elenor?"

"God yeah, a right dirty old cow I bet," he conjectured, giving my mixed feelings a quick stir. "You can always tell."

"I can see Elenor with three geezers more than I can see Sally with three geezers," I told him.

"I can see both of them with three geezers – couple of slags," Tom informed me, taking a considered puff on his cigarette. "Anyway, you don't want to worry about that, dirty nooky ain't all it's cracked up to be. And after one or two rounds the appeal's gone anyway so that all you're left with is a big load of guilt and a skeleton that'll rattle around in your cupboard for the rest of your life. Honestly mate, it ain't worth it."

"I know. At least I know now," I agreed, and I did. As sexy as I found Elenor, I also found her seriously annoying. I just hadn't been able to see that side of her for a few weeks because my horn kept obscuring the view. A bucket of cold reality in the face and I suddenly couldn't understand why I'd even wanted her in my room.

"So what's she been like since the party?"

"A little bit offish actually. She hasn't said anything about it so I figure it's best left alone."

"Probably annoyed at you for turning her down. Girls like Elenor don't like to be turned down," Tom surmised. "They're not used to it."

I had thought about pulling her to one side to talk to her but when I saw how funny she was being with me I decided to take the coward's way out and simply put up my own set of shutters. Chuck Godfrey not talking to me in the mix, the rest of the Xtremers glaring at me because my mate had got their mate fired and Norman popping around every five minutes to bang on about his fucking report and I can't tell you what a joy work was at the moment.

"Still, look on the bright side," Tom said. "You'll probably never get another chance with Elenor, not now that you fucked this one up. That's the rule. Blokes only ever get one shot at a girl and if you don't take it there and then, a lifetime of trying will never present you with another," he reckoned, making me remember my near-miss with Abigail all those regret-filled years ago.

"Hmm," I agreed.

"Cheer up mate, that's a good thing," Tom said, when he saw the look his last insight had left on my face.

"Yeah. Yeah, I know it is," I conceded.

"Don't worry, just think, this time next year, you'll be a dad. Then you'll really know what problems are all about," Tom winked.

Sally's Diary: February 12th

I'M SO EXCITED about my news that I want to tell everyone, but I still haven't had my scan and until I do I mustn't say a word. But you've no idea how hard that is.

I can't make up my mind if Andrew's taking it all in his stride or is contemplating doing a runner. He certainly seems to have a few anxieties he's not letting me in on because he looks positively stilted every time we talk about it. Not so much the proud father who's impregnated his wife as the guilty little pooch who's pooed somewhere you're yet to find.

But I couldn't be more excited if I tried. I drift off to sleep every night dreaming about my baby. Being with him or her. Taking care of him or her and smothering them in love. It feels so right that I can't understand why we waited this long. A whole new chapter of my life is opening up before me and I suddenly feel complete. My God, if this is how I feel after only ten weeks, what am I going to feel like when my baby actually arrives? I know it's an over-used expression but it really feels like I have a miracle growing inside me. And all those children I've taught over the years, and all the children in the other classes, other schools and other countries, they all must've brought the same feelings into the world with them.

Amazing then how the world's not a nicer place isn't it?

CHAPTER 13.
BUT THEN SOMETHING AWFUL HAPPENED…

SALLY GOT HER period.

It came out of the blue because up until this point she'd been utterly utterly utterly convinced she'd been pregnant. It was something that Sally just hadn't expected.

"Come on love, don't fret it. After all, we hadn't planned that one anyway," I said in an ill-conceived attempt to cheer her up. I then went on to compare her false alarm to finding twenty quid in the street, only to realise it had fallen out of your own pocket in the first place.

Not my finest hour.

So I tried to gee her up with a couple of Nicole Kidman movies and an industrial-sized box of Maltesers which did the trick for a couple of nights…

But then something really awful happened.

Sally continued to feel nauseous and bloated for another week or so, prompting her to seek a second opinion in case she actually was still pregnant. And that's when it was confirmed to us that she wasn't.

No, Sally actually had cancer.

It smacks you right in the face when you say it, doesn't it? But that was the fact of the matter. Sally had cancer. Or at least, suspected cancer. Ovarian to be precise.

We had it confirmed a couple of days later after Sally went up for tests and something called a transvaginal ultrasound screening. We'd tried to take our minds off the worst by joking about the name, with Sally reckoning it sounded like Dracula's music system or something, but the joking stopped when the screening actually found something.

What a nightmare! And one that had an effect on me that of a thousand buckets of cold water couldn't have matched, dislodging all remaining thoughts of Elenor from my brain. Though these would later come back to haunt me.

At first, I couldn't take it in because cancer wasn't something young school teachers got. Cancer was something hell-raising movie legends got after a lifetime of booze and broads. At the very least, it was something your great Auntie Ada got and was perfectly all right about. *"Don't worry about me, I've had a good innings. Just see to it that my cats are well taken care of and I'll leave you all my money. What's that? Why yes, I do have an old Hessian sack and a couple of bricks. Why do you ask?"*

But young, intelligent, kind and caring school teachers? What was all that about?

At first, it was so much to take in that both Sally and I chose to bury our heads in the sand. We didn't go as far and kidding ourselves that there was nothing wrong at all, but we opted to believe it wasn't anything serious; a tiny little polyp, small and insignificant, that could be batted away as easily as a fly and wasn't it lucky we found it at an early stage?

But until the doctors took a good look inside Sally, we wouldn't know for sure. And that was probably the hardest part. The waiting. Days dragged their heels like you wouldn't believe and neither of us dared to speculate as to the extent of Sally's disease for fear of letting it into our minds.

It was a terrible week. I decided I couldn't just sit still, so I got myself down the local library and started reading up on the enemy. Here are a few facts I found out which I want share with you before we go on any further.

There are four stages of ovarian cancer – stage I being the earliest and stage IV being the last. In addition to this, there are three classifications for each stage – A, B and C (C being the least desirable). Then you have the grades for the tumours themselves – grade I, II and III, indicating what sort of mood the tumour's in and let's not forget the strain of the cancer itself.

There are six main variants of ovarian cancer; serous, mucinous, endometrioid, clear cell and a couple of others I jotted down, but unfortunately can't read back. I thought I would be able to handle it from an academic point of view but after only half an hour of horror, my handwriting could've passed for Guy Fawkes' final note to the milkman.

Ovarian cancer on the whole, was the fourth most common form of cancer in women though the survival rate was sadly poor when compared with other cancers.

See, the thing is, if you caught it early, like with all cancers, you could pretty much root it out and eradicate it with surgery and drugs. But ovarian cancer's tricky because it's hidden away and the symptoms and signals it gives off can be so easily misconstrued. Lots of women dismiss their disease as heartburn or even indigestion. Sally dismissed hers as a baby, something Queen Mary I did too back in 1558, much to her and the newly rejuvenated Catholic England's dismay. As a matter of fact, the most common way in which ovarian cancer is usually discovered is when couples go in for IVF treatment and the scan turns up the reason they're having difficulties.

See, the trouble is, there's no screening test for ovarian cancer – unlike pap smears or mamogram tests for cervical and breast cancers, so more often than not the little bastard's already set up home before anyone knows he's in there. Hence the poor survival rate.

And ovarian cancer's nickname as the silent killer.

Look, I think I'm going to stop there, not least of all because I don't want to turn this into *The Vagina Monologues*. I just wanted to fill in a little detail and put you into the picture as to what sort of foe we were up against.

We? Okay, Sally.

*

"Am I going to die?" Sally asked the doctor.

"People hear the word cancer and they immediately think the worst, but in reality there are lots and lots of women with quite progressive cancers, who live with their disease for many years," the doctor replied, sounding half like he meant it too. "Now, we're going to get things moving right away and book you in with the oncologist. This means we'll need to perform a surgical procedure called a staging laparotomy, just to take a peek inside you and then debulk the main affected areas. We'll send anything we find away for analysis then consider what further treatment, if any, is required when we get the results back. Okay?"

This all sounded okay to me, but then again I wasn't the one who was going to die.

I managed to remove my hand from Sally's long enough to dig out my handkerchief, but she looked up at me in surprise and even managed a smirk when she felt how wringing wet it already was.

"Sorry," I coughed, doing my best to run through all the brick walls of emotion to be strong for my wife.

"Now, if it is only a small tumour on one ovary, then we may have to remove that ovary. If, however, the cancer has spread, then this may involve a hysterectomy, so it's important that you understand the full implications of this procedure," the doctor said, as scarily as possible.

He then went on to expand on the implications and Sally

squeezed my hand so tightly that the doctor had to take a quick look at it before we left with all our unvoiced questions still bouncing around our brains.

"I'm really scared," Sally said, shivering in my arms in the early spring chill once we were outside.

"It's okay. Honestly, it'll be okay," I tried to reassure her, though what I was basing that on was anyone's guess. Still, it seemed more helpful than rattling her by the arms and screaming into her face, "Me too. Oh God, what the fuck are we going to do?"

"Why us? What have we done to deserve this?" Sally swallowed, leaning against the car for support.

"Nothing, love. Absolutely nothing. I don't think it works like that," I told her, shaking my head when I thought about all the terrorists, torturers and playboys out there who were walking around smug and cancer-free. "Besides, you heard what the doctor said, there are thousands of women who have well progressed cancers who are still able to live perfectly normal lives."

"I didn't hear him say thousands," Sally pointed out.

"Didn't he? Well that's what he meant. I don't think he would've mentioned it if there was only one or two. Look, all you need to know is that these people are experts. They know what they're doing and they're going to get you better. I don't even have any doubts," I promised. I was about to expand on this point but Sally cut me short by burying her head into my neck and bursting into tears.

"I'm sorry. I'm sorry. I'm sorry," she just kept blubbing irrationally, over and over again. Several hospital visitors looked our way, but none of them lingered long enough to intrude on the moment.

"There there. There there," I muttered, rubbing her back

and doing all I could to soothe her shakes.

*

Incredibly, Norman absolutely insisted I took a week's compassionate leave to be with Sally when she went in for her surgery and this was even more astonishing when you considered that he'd already been covering for Tom for the past five weeks. I asked him if he was sure he could do both magazines and Norman assured me that the work load was no problem and that he was actually enjoying getting his hands dirty again after so long in "the big office".

I was a little wary of him covering for us both, because I was worried he'd see how little actual work there was to do, but then Tom pointed out that Norman had a full-time job at the company too and no one was covering for him while he was playing in our seats so what could he say?

Anyway, it was a nice thing for Norman to do and I couldn't help but feel bad for some of the things I'd said about him in the past.

*

The days leading up to the laparotomy were a whirlwind of conflicting emotions. Sally was both anxious about her surgery and frantic to have it done. Every hour she went without treatment was another hour the enemy had to grow.

Sally wanted it out and she wanted to be free. But most of all, I sensed, she wanted not to be scared any more.

She felt particularly bitter towards her cancer because of the deception it had pulled. She'd showered her little miracle with love and hope for almost a month before the doctors had told her the truth and the betrayal was nothing short of cruel. It knocked Sally for six and left her helpless as a kitten, so I took it upon myself to be her one-man support network and made sure I was never further than a groan away. As it turned out, it only took me a couple of days to realise why there wasn't a queue of volunteers stretching around the block for this particular job.

"What?"

"Tea. Can you make me a cup of tea?" she flapped wearily.

"Another one? You had one only twenty minutes ago."

"No, I didn't drink it and it went cold," she said, pointing to a full cup of tea by the side of her bed.

"Well, do you want me to put it in the microwave for thirty seconds then? Warm it up?"

"Urgh no, I don't like it like that."

"It doesn't make any difference, it'll just warm it up."

"No, it makes it taste funny. Oh don't worry about it then," she heaved miserably, her body language lamenting *first cancer, now this*.

"No no, I'll make you one if you want one," I insisted, finally leaping into action.

"No, don't bother. I don't think I want one now."

"It's all right, it's no bother."

"Just forget it," she grumbled.

I bit my tongue, counted to three and went and made Sally a cup of tea anyway. As I was doing so Tom wheeled himself over to see how we were doing.

"How are you Sugar?" Tom asked, his nickname for her at university. Sally replied by bursting into tears and leaning on his wheelchair so hard I had to grab one of the armrests to prevent them from both rolling out of the house.

"Not bad," she finally croaked, a big brave smile across her face. "How are you?"

"Getting better with every passing day. You'll see what that's like soon enough," he winked.

Sally's Diary: March 15th

I'M HAVING my surgery this morning and I'm scared. I know it's a standard procedure but I'm still worried. I'm sorry to admit this but I've always been a coward when it comes to doctors. I know there are people in other parts of the world that have more to be scared about than me right now but I can't help myself. Injections, examinations, stitches and operations; they all bring me out in a cold sweat. A few years ago, I cried the morning I had to have two wisdom teeth out. God, I wish I were having two wisdom teeth out today. I'd give anything to be having two wisdom teeth out today. I'm scared of the anaesthetic. I'm scared of the drip. I'm scared of having to just lie there and let a lot of people in masks take scalpels to me. And I'm scared of what they might find when they do.

I have such a longing to run and hide but there's nowhere I can run to because the thing I long to run from is inside of me. I'm scared of all of these things and more. But most of all that the cancer has spread. Because if that has happened…

It's not fair. It's just not fair…

CHAPTER 14.
HOSPITAL CAFETERIAS AND OTHER STRANGE PLACES

I TRIED TO smother Sally with as much reassurance as I could but I don't know if any of it got through. Actually I think I just made myself more nervous. Sally looked so small and so helpless amongst all those grown-ups that ten years of lost love caught up with me like a rocket-powered boxing glove. Actually, that's not true. My love for Sally was never lost, it had just taken a wrong turning a few years back and had got sidetracked looking through lingerie shop windows.

"Right then, come along. I'm afraid I'm going to have to ask you to leave us now," the nurse informed me in a way that made me want to suck my thumb. "Say goodbye and then go and get yourself a cup of tea. Don't worry, your wife will be fine with us and you'll see her later."

I stopped my bottom lip wobbling just long enough to press it against Sally's and told her one last time that everything would be okay before I was finally ejected out into the hospital corridor.

My last glimpse of Sally was of her nervously unbuttoning her cardigan as the nurse busied herself around the bed. When the door finally clicked shut I stared at it for about a minute and suppressed the urge to start barking. But then the door opened again and I almost collided heads with the nurse when I tried to look inside for another quick peek.

"Come on now, shoo, shoo, off you go," she insisted, pushing me back away from the door and verbally clipping me around the ear. "Your wife is in the best of hands. Now go and get yourself a cup of tea."

A cup of tea was possibly about the last thing in the world I wanted but I knew I had to get out from under their feet, so I decided to play ball and go and do the thing we English did best in times of crisis.

"Where do I get a cup of tea from?" I asked the nurse.

"From the cafeteria. Down the corridor and turn left, through the doors, down the stairs and follow it round. You can't miss it," she replied, though twenty minutes of blundering around the corridors of the hospital proved she was no judge of orienteer.

Still, at least it gave me something else to think about and for that I was marginally grateful.

As I searched for this mythical cafeteria, I couldn't help but wonder at how brave Sally was being. I'd never liked hospitals myself. I mean, who does? But they'd always scared the bejesus out of me in particular. In the movies, hospitals were usually crisp, clean places, where concerned doctors outnumbered the patients five-to-one and dramatic music and beeping life support machines conveniently glossed over the cacophony of coughing and constant buzz of unanswered telephones.

Outside of the movies, hospitals were frighteningly real places. In fact, they were the most real places on Earth. And the long, bright corridors and cold, hard fixtures just underlined this every blundering footstep of the way.

Radiology. Anaesthetics. Cystic Fibrosis. Diabetes. Dietetics. Special Care Baby Unit. Teenage Unit. Physiotherapy. Intensive Care Unit. Accident & Emergency. Cancer Unit.

These signs were posted in every corridor and on every stair well and they all scared me to tears although the scariest of these had to be Chaplaincy. About the only sign they didn't have was Cafeteria, so I kept on searching until I found an equally lost soul staring up at a big board of signs.

"Excuse me, but do you know where the cafeteria is?" the old boy asked as I stopped to examine the board myself.

"Hopefully somewhere near Frimley," I replied, this being Frimley Park Hospital.

"Yes, it's a bit tricky isn't it," the old fella agreed.

By lucky chance, my new friend managed to snag a passing nurse and we squeezed a new set of directions out of her, which seemed to involve returning to Go and starting again.

"Do you think they've actually got a cafeteria here?" the chap asked, as the clatter of the nurse's brogues faded down the hospital corridor.

"Perhaps we should've got her to draw a map," I replied.

"Hmm, yes. Well, do you want to see if we can find it together?" he offered and to my surprise I found myself saying yes.

The old boy looked almost twice my age but good with it. His shirt was ironed, his shoes were polished and his jacket was pressed. He was also clean-shaven and combed, whereas I was none of these things. I had four-day stubble, flyaway hair, a jumper that looked like it had last been worn by *The Thing* and a jacket that had less of an idea where the dry cleaners was than I did.

I guess one of us had been in the army when we were younger. Or at least, had come from a generation whose Sunday dress was Sunday best, not tattered old jogging bottoms and an egg-stained T-shirt.

"This looks the ticket," he said, when we finally spied a Cafeteria sign. We followed subsequent signs through one last corridor before finally locating the tinkle of cutlery and the squeaking of chairs.

"Can I get you a cup of tea?" he offered before I had the chance to do likewise.

"Please, thank you," I replied, and found us both a table.

He brought us back a tray of all the various bits and bobs they give you whenever you buy a cup of tea in a cafeteria and we settled either side of each other and poured the contents all over the table.

"I can never get the hang of these blasted tin spouts," he replied, frowning at his little metal pot and mopping up the worst of the spillage with a napkin. "Are you here visiting someone?"

"Yes, I've come with my wife," I replied, then almost choked when I said the words, "she's got cancer."

"Oh, I'm very sorry to hear that," he sympathised and even though he didn't press I ended up telling him all about her condition and all about her operation until all the tea was gone. "I see," he said.

"I just don't know what to do," I ended up sniffing.

"Yes, it's difficult," he agreed, then thought for a moment. "You just have to do what you can I suppose. You're not a doctor I take it?"

"No."

"Or a, what do they call those chaps, a radiographer?"

"No."

"And you certainly don't look like a nurse," he pointed out, also pointing out the attitudes of the decade he seemed to have wandered in from. "So you just have to do what you can," he said. "It might not seem much at first, but it's the little things that make all the difference. Look after her. Take care of her. Cook her dinner. Bring her flowers. Make her feel special. Your wife, what's her name?"

"Sally."

"Sally needs a friend right now and the best friend a woman can have is her husband."

"And vice versa?"

"Without doubt," he nodded. "Without doubt."

His eyes sparkled a moment to suggest his thoughts were elsewhere and I was about to ask his own circumstances when he got in first and asked me if Sally was my actual wife, or whether she was just my common-law wife.

"No, my actual wife. We were married seven years ago," I told him, my mind drifting back to that gloriously hot summers day.

"Good," he approved. "A lot of people don't these days so you can never tell. You remember those words; for better, for worse, in sickness and in health and all the rest of them?"

"I do," I replied. The old fella smiled.

"Well, you just have to do your best to live up to that vow. For richer, for better, in health? These are the easy ones to live up to, but for poorer, for worse and in sickness? They're what marriage is really all about. To be there for each other."

At this point, a sniff turned into a blub, which turned into a shudder, which turned into tears and before I could slam on the brakes, the boo-hoo express was pulling into the station. Everything was on top of me. Everything. Sally's pain. What the doctors might find. My uselessness.

And my shame over what had almost transpired with Elenor.

"It's a difficult thing to be strong for someone else," my elderly friend said. "You just have to try. You just have to be optimistic."

"It's not that," I finally admitted, barely able to look him in the eye.

"What is it then? Tell me."

But I couldn't. He was a decent, kind, old man, who'd clearly been best friends with his wife their whole lives, whereas I was the scum of the Earth who'd almost hopped into bed with my secretary while my wife had been stricken with cancer (not that I knew it at the time).

Eventually I got this off my chest, if only to necessitate the scorn I duly deserved, but the old boy simply nodded some more.

"I see," he said again.

He handed me a napkin and I wiped my eyes and blew my nose until I could almost breathe in silence again then he told me I shouldn't take on so.

"You didn't go with this girl then, this Elenor, did you?" he asked. I shook my head and told him I hadn't. "Have you ever been unfaithful with any other woman?" he then asked. Again, I told him I hadn't. "There you go then. That's good, very good in fact. Don't be so hard on yourself."

"But that's not the point. I almost did and that's the thing I can't get over."

"You can't beat yourself up over every little thing you almost did, young fella," he said. "It's hard enough coping with the things we actually do without piling on the pressure of the things we almost do as well. I mean if you think about it, it's better to be tempted and pass temptation than to never be tempted at all."

The old boy thought for a moment then leaned in a little closer.

"You know, I almost killed my daughter one time," he said, making me stare up at him in horror. "Oh it was an accident and everything, but it would've still amounted to the same thing," he sighed, shaking his head forlornly. "I was up on the roof see, replacing a couple of broken slates. I was a bit sprightlier back then of course. I was also a bit more impulsive. I had all my tools and materials up there with me and once I'd finished I started clearing everything away. So, what did I do? Like an idiot I started throwing the old slates and bits of baton and even my tools into the lawn below, hammer and screwdriver and saw and so on, to save myself a couple of trips up and down the ladder. Naturally, I'd called down to make sure no one was below, but the kitchen door was open and my calls lured my six year old out to see what all the fuss was about."

The old boy paused and blinked a couple of times in disbelief.

"One of the broken slates brushed her head by fractions of an inch. It came so close, in fact, that the corner actually took the tiniest little nick out of her scalp. That was how close I came to killing my daughter," he said, staring back at the memory. "Still makes me shudder," he puffed, blowing out his cheeks and shaking his head. "All to save three or four trips up a twenty foot ladder."

"Was she okay?"

"Oh right as rain, except for a little cut in her hair. She works in London now, something to do with the interweb or something, I don't know."

"But that was just an accident," I said.

"No, it was *almost* an accident," he corrected me. "Actually, I like to think of it more as a lucky escape; miraculous even, and one I've said thanks for every day since. I know it might not seem like the same thing but think about it anyway."

"I will," I promised him, trying to sound like I meant it.

"I'll tell you another thing, I don't throw bloody crap off the roof any more either," he laughed. "Righto, well it was nice to meet you Andrew. I really hope your wife gets better.

She sounds like a smashing young lady. Well, all the best."

The old boy rose to leave when I suddenly realised I'd been so busy talking about myself that I hadn't even bothered asking him his circumstances.

"Me? Oh I'm here with the wife too. In-growing toenails. Can you believe it? At her age? I told her not to wear those shoes." And with that, he gave me one last smile, then disappeared off into the labyrinth of hospital corridors.

A nice old man.

With more slates than he knew.

Sally's Diary: March 17th

Too sad…

CHAPTER 15.
TEST RESULTS

IT WAS THE news we'd been dreading and it pushed us beyond emotional pain barriers we never even knew existed.

Sally's cancer had spread.

Tests and the staging laparotomy confirmed that it was stage II B grade I 'Serous' ovarian cancer, for those of you who like to get technical about these sorts of things.

I'm able to give you the full name for it now because I've had time to get over my initial shock and actually take some of it in, but at the time it was just a jumble of words. Scary algebra for doctors and it left me on the floor when we were told the results.

In fact, when I first heard these words an icy hand gripped my heart and squeezed it with such force that I thought I might black out. And I probably would've done too had it not been for the fact that I was meant to be there for Sally, not the other way around. With everything else on her plate, the last thing she needed was me falling face first into the tiles to sidetrack the conversation.

Still, at least we now knew its name. As it happened, Serous is the most common variant of Ovarian cancer, so this was something at the very least. Well, if you've got to get cancer it's probably best to get the most common form of it rather than the extremely rare type that only you and really fucking unlucky foothill pigmy's get, don't you think? The most common and the most widely researched.

The doctor went on.

While they had successfully debulked a considerable proportion of the affected areas, subsequent tests showed that further treatment was going to be needed.

This meant chemotherapy.

A few strides had been made in recent years with regards chemotherapy. A new drug had come over from America called Taxol which when administered alongside other drugs gave for a better survival rate.

I didn't like the words, "survival rate," but I quickly came to realise these were the terms in which cancer was spoken. Survival. Five years to be precise.

That didn't mean that the doctors would help Sally live for five years then that was her lot.

"All done, off you go, you're on your own." It was just a scientific way of measuring the immeasurable and as good a way as anyone had come up with thus far.

Commonly, for women with Stage I ovarian cancer, there was a seventy-eight per cent survival rate. For women like Sally, with Stage II, this dropped to fifty-nine per cent. Stage III dropped even further to twenty-three per cent and for women with Stage IV, only fourteen per cent would still be with us in five years.

Naturally, like with everything in life, there were no concrete equations and you had to take into account a myriad of considerations with each individual case but by and large Sally had roughly a three in five chance of surviving until she was forty.

Fortunately for Sally, she had a number of factors going in her favour. She was young and she was strong, so the doctors were optimistic that she'd respond well to the chemo, though this was going to be a testing ordeal for her.

These were powerful drugs and they were going to make her pretty ill. I mean chemotherapy is basically a poison. Localised and targeted, it's poison nevertheless, which is used to stop a part of your body that's growing out of control in its tracks. This is what chemotherapy boils down to.

"So, you're going to have to build up your strength. Diet is very important, as are plenty of rest, exercise and support."

Then the doctor looked at me for some reason.

"Family and friends have never been so important as they are now. I can get you some literature on the subject that'll help you help Sally," he said.

Unable to remember which words I was supposed to use at this particular juncture in my life, I just nodded and expressed as much unhappy gratitude as I could.

Sally barely looked up.

See, while the news was positive as far as her survival chances were concerned, there was more to it than that. The cancer had spread to her other ovary, her fallopian tubes and her uterus.

The doctors had cut it all out and were happy they'd caught it in time.

But Sally would never have children.

Sally's Diary: March 18th

I DON'T know how to describe what I'm feeling today because it's too big an emotion to deal with. It's too huge. Too all consuming. There's hardly anything of me left. I'm almost completely gone. Too much. Andrew's coming later.

Sally's Diary: March 19th

NO APPETITE. *And not just for food. I can't read or watch TV or listen to music or make conversation. Everything is a horrible irritation. I'm going to try to put into words how I'm feeling because Andrew thinks it might help. I don't know about that but it's marginally more preferable to spending the day staring at my bottom lip.*

Feel sick.

I've never known anyone who's died before. A girl who was in the same English class as me at school did and both sets of grandparents have passed away but I don't think I ever spoke more than six words to the girl at school (they were "are we in this classroom today?") and I was too young to remember my grandparents. But that's what this feels like – mourning. I'm mourning my babies. I'm mourning their loss. I'll never see their faces or hold them or tell them that I love them or...

Headache.

The nurse brought me a flannel for my face and it felt so good that I forgot about everything except that flannel. I got another one for my stitches and lay beneath them groaning until the novelty wore off.

Sore.

I'm full of emptiness. Choked to the point of bursting and there's nothing I can do to relieve the pressure. I know I should eat something but I can't. Managed some soup but brought it back up little on.

I always thought I'd have children one day. Like rain during a long hot summer. The weeks might stretch on and on but you know it'll rain one day. It will because it has to. One day. You just take it for granted. But now it won't. It'll never happen. How has this happened?

Andrew brought me magazines but I can't fix my eyes on the words. Nothing's soaking in. And don't have the energy to try.

Tired.

Sally's Diary: March 20th

THIS DAY looks a lot like yesterday only it's raining outside. It's lashing against the windows in thick, whipping sheets and drawing everyone's eyes. It feels like the sky is crying and reflecting my mood with its great black clouds. It's miserable outside and it's miserable in here. Everything is black and white. Andrew's coming later. That's all I have to say about today.

Sally's Diary: March 21st

A new woman arrived this morning and they put her in next to me. She tried to strike up a conversation but I didn't feel like talking so she spent the entire morning talking to the lady in the bed opposite. The nurse asked them to keep it down but they carried on regardless. I can't help but soak it all up in the absence of any other sort of distraction and now I know everything there is to know about her; where she lives, what her husband does, what her children are called, what programs she likes on TV and what sort of carpet they have in their living room. She just goes on and on.

The moment she saw me writing she asked me what I was doing and then spent the next twenty minutes telling me about how she used to keep a diary when she was a little girl and how her mother found it and so on until I fell asleep. I actually fell asleep while she was talking. She looked hurt when I woke up and has left me alone since. I want to go home. I want my own bed. I want to be with Andrew.

Sally's Diary: March 22nd

I KEEP wondering if something can be done. If there hasn't been a mistake. Pinpricks of hope keep tricking me into grasping at beautiful straws because I can't bring myself to believe the reality. It's too cruel. And I fall for it every time. Because I want to fall for it. Because I don't want it to be true. "Great news Mrs Nolan, it's a one in a hundred shot but with the technology we've got today it is just possible we could..." etc. But no doctors have come with such news and I don't think any doctor's going to. Because there is no way back. And all the technology in the world isn't going to fix me. I expect in fifty years times they'll be able to do something about it but that won't help me. I'm here, I'm now and I'm all alone. At least until Andrew comes tonight.

Sally's Diary: March 23rd

THIS SHOULD be my last day on the ward. The doctor is coming to see me a little later on and hopefully he'll let me go home. I'm trying to eat all my meals and put a smile on my face but it's difficult. Thoughts occur to me at my lowest moments that I know I shouldn't entertain them but I can't help it.

See it's easy to forget that while this has happened to me, it's also happened to Andrew too. He'll never be a father. He'll never kick a ball with his son or hold his daughter's hand. He'll never know what it is to have a family. And like me he'll always wonder what might have been.

What must Andrew be going through? What must he be feeling?

Because of course this only applies if he stays with me...

But what a terrible thing to think about one's husband! That he could do such a thing. But if he did what would it say about me if I tried standing in his way?

This is such a cruel disease. The doctors did their best to cut it all out. But it's still with me, playing its malicious games of deceit.

CHAPTER 16.
ALL WOMAN

"HOW AM I meant to make sure she eats properly when she's hardly eating at all?" I asked Tom as I cleared out the last of the kitchen cupboards. I put all the unwanted jars, tins and packets in a box and let Tom take what he liked – which was everything. "Saves me a shop," he explained.

He was particularly taken with the four bottles of red wine I was throwing out and suggested we opened one now and had a drink.

"But what if she needs me for something?"

"Fuck me mate, I said a drink, not a drinking contest. Christ come on, stop staring at the stairs every five minutes and have a cup of wine. If ever I saw a man who needed alcohol, I'm looking at one right now."

Tom fished one of the bottles of Merlot back out of the box and opened it up (although not the nice one I noticed). He poured us two generous glasses and raised his to Sally, who'd come home this afternoon.

"To Sally," I repeated and we drank to her health.

"So, she's not allowed any alcohol at all then?"

"Alcohol's a poison too. And she's having to put up with enough of that already, what with the chemo, so it's total detox all the way."

"Cheese as well?" he said, picking out a packet of stilton.

"All dairy products really. And red meat. Big no-nos. See, digesting this stuff uses up enzymes that are needed for fighting the cancer," I explained, flipping through one of the many leaflets the doctor had given me and pointing to the paragraph to prove I hadn't just made this up.

"Yeah, but why are you chucking it out? You ain't got cancer."

"Ow come on, what am I going to do, sit here getting legless and eating cheese on toast in front of her while her hair falls out?" I told him.

"So, what's in and what's out?"

"Basically everything we've ever eaten up to now," I sighed, frowning at my empty cupboards. "Red meat, white bread, black tea, coffee, sugary drinks, salt, curry, white rice, sweets, chips and pretty much anything processed, plus vitamin E, ginseng, alcohol and tap water."

"I bet you're gutted about the ginseng, aren't you?" he nodded.

"The things we're able to eat; as much fresh fruit and vegetables as we can, preferably organic, brown rice, wholegrain bread, pulses, beans, and seeds. A bit of free-range chicken, though not too much, organic fish, again a couple of ounces, plus garlic, a little bit of soy, the odd egg here and there and lots of water."

"Bottled?" Tom speculated.

"Well, it's not ideal. I mean, who knows how many nuclear power plants the lorry driver's driven past on his way over from France. No, they recommend you fit something called an osmosis water filter to your water system and boil it all if you can and make it pure and all that, for best results."

"And are you?"

"Should be here at the end of the week," I said.

"All this stuff must be expensive. You know, water pumps and organic food and all that."

"Yeah well, let's just say we're dipping into the kids' college fund with a clear conscience these days."

"Oh. Sorry mate," Tom grimaced. "Is Sally still in a bad

way about that?"

I took the bottle off Tom and topped up both our glasses.

"She's always wanted kids. Me too, come to that, but it was always one of those things that we were going to do when the time was right. Next year. Maybe the year after that. Don't worry there's plenty of time, we're young and nobody has kids until they're in their thirties these days anyway. Sally's only thirty-four and now the time's never going to be right. Ever. It's something I don't think she'll ever get over."

Tom said nothing. Perhaps there was nothing to be said.

I'd found all the above out when the doctors had broken the news to Sally in her hospital bed. It was the thing she'd feared most and the thing for which there were no possible words of comfort. It was without doubt the worst moment of my life. I can't even begin to glimpse how terrible it must've been for Sally.

What a dreadful, dreadful day.

"I just don't know what to do. And I don't know how to make her better, because she's never going to be better," I welled, fighting to suppress my tattered emotions in front of a mate. I wiped my eye and drank my drink, then apologised. Tom told me not to be such a dickhead. For a moment, I thought he meant I was being a dickhead because I was on the verge of tears, which I remember thinking was a bit harsh, even by Tom's standards, before realising he meant for apologising.

"You know the ridiculous thing," I said, when I found my voice again. "Is that Sally keeps calling herself half a woman. I mean, it's ridiculous, isn't it?"

"It's like a bloke calling himself half a man because he gets his nuts shot off, I guess. Amounts to the same thing," Tom reckoned.

"I don't know. Maybe, whatever it is though, it's ridiculous."

And I couldn't have meant that more. For me, never more than this moment, Sally was the epitome of womanhood. She was kind, she was pretty, she was affectionate and caring and in need. And I so desperately wanted to take care of her and lavish her with love and devotion for the rest of my life.

I know that description of womanhood might not go down that well with the nutty Labour fatties in the local Town Hall, who'd like nothing better than to see me and my car clapped in irons for expressing such an outrageous opinion, but they could go to hell on a broom handle as far as I was concerned. I was all out of political correctness and patience for anyone who was anything other than a help to Sally and bollocks to anyone who wasn't.

"And what about you?" Tom then asked.

"What about me?"

"How do you feel about all this? About the possibility of never having children?"

Tom let that question linger in the air so that I'd spot the significance of what he was getting at and I could think of only one way of answering him.

"If Sally doesn't eat ginseng, then I don't get to eat ginseng either," I told him.

<u>Sally's Diary: March 24th</u>

MY HOME looks unnervingly spotless, almost like it's not my home. Andrew has definitely been working on his OCD while I've been away and has even taken to folding the ends of the toilet roll into a little arrow. As far as the rest of the house is concerned, this evening I'm going to eat my supper off that bit of floor behind the fridge, simply because these days I can, and afterwards I'm going to spend the rest of the evening scouring the house for our last surviving germ.

I've also decided to expose Andrew for the charlatan he is and collapse unexpectedly to try to catch him out. If I do this a hundred times I think it's safe to say he'll not be hovering at my side to catch me at least once. Maybe.

I shouldn't mock, he means well and he's working so hard. And everything he's done he's done for me, but he must be exhausted. I know I am and that's just from watching him. It's so good to be home again that I've almost remembered what colour happiness is. In fact it feels such a relief that I've decided to make a concerted effort not to be unhappy any longer, because it's doing neither of us any good, least of all Andrew. I need to take what good I can from this situation and stop concentrating on the negative. It's important — for both of us. After all, if the orchestra can play Abide With Me as the Titanic goes down, why can't I play Monopoly with Andrew?

CHAPTER 17.
FOOD FOR THOUGHT

YOU KNOW, it's bananas when you think about all the crap we eat (bananas perhaps not being the best example). I was thinking about this the other day after my first couple of organic dinners and it's no wonder we're all ill and fat and dying from different diseases.

See, with me, I used to be one of those blokes who would look down his nose and sneer at vegans and vegetarians and organic fanatics and such like and dismiss them all with one regal wave of the chip fork as idiot nut-jobs, tree-huggers and sissies. I mean, what was wrong with a bit of bacon? And not just bacon; steak, chicken, bangers and mash? Baked beans, fried eggs, white bread and butter? Mince pies, pork pies, sausage rolls and pasties? Cheeseburgers, hamburgers, fish fingers and chips? Roast lamb, tinned soup, corned beef and gateau?

And that's not even including all the condiments we splatter on top of our dinners the moment they're laid in front of us.

Salt, pepper, mustard and ketchup. White sauce, brown sauce, mint sauce and vinegar. Mayonnaise, salad cream, tartar and chilli. Raspberry sauce, chocolate sauce, custard and cream. And if that's not enough to get our dinners tasting okay, heaps and heaps of sugar and a couple of chocolate flakes.

It gives my guts somersaults just thinking about it all.

See, I was thinking that we are actually a very finely balanced organism. I know we all like to think we're hard as nails and can handle a hand grenade vindaloo and ten pints of Kingfisher no problem, but really we can't. Not regularly. Not without doing ourselves untold damage.

Not even Geordies.

See, we are the end product of millions and millions of years of fine tinkering by Mother Nature. Evolution. That's the word I was looking for.

We have, as a species, evolved over millions and millions of years to become the animal we are today. That is, unless you believe in God, in which case we only took the click of a couple of big fingers and were something of an afterthought as it was (Eve even more so than Adam). But let's forget about God for the time being because He completely undoes all my theories.

So evolution.

This is an incredibly gradual process. It takes millions and millions of years and only ends when a species becomes extinct. Nature doesn't sit still, but then by that same token she doesn't exactly break any speed records either, because change is a dangerous thing and it usually takes a great deal of time to bed down. Consequently we're a very finely balanced animal. As indeed every animal is.

I heard someone on the telly once say that evolution takes into account three things – diet, environment and culture, and I can totally believe this, especially about the diet and environment. See, the way I reckon it is this: if you took my old friend caveman Ug from fifty thousand years ago and some olde worlde John Bull yeoman off the land from two hundred years ago, sat them down and gave them a couple of medicals – and I mean the works – I bet you'd find that there wasn't much between them. Yeah sure, one of them might have bigger teeth, more hair and fingernails he could scratch his feet with while standing upright but I bet you'd hardly be able to tell their livers, hearts, kidneys and lungs apart. And that's because, if you think about it, life has hardly changed for either of these blokes and everyone in between for thousands of years. They both breathed the same air, drank the same water and ate pretty much the same foods (fruit, veg, grain and meat – all organic) and they both toiled and sweated for their daily bread.

But you can't say that about us today.

The air we breathe has crap and pollutants in it that were never around in either Ug or John Bull's day. The same goes for the water and the land we cultivate on. Pesticides, chemicals and toxins. And that's not even mentioning all the microwaves, ultrawaves, radiation and mobile phone masts cooking our brains twenty-four hours a day. Then there's the food; additives, colourings, preservatives, enhancers, monosodium glutamates and rehomogenisation. What the hell is homogenisation? And why the hell does it have to be done twice? And to my dinner? Genetic engineering, intensive farming, cross pollination, best before dates and brown sauce.

All of these things are suddenly being put into bodies that have grown strong off the back of a stable fifty thousand-year-old diet. This has to be a shock to the system.

The question shouldn't be why are we all getting fat and unhealthy and filling cancer wards all of the time; it should be why are some of us getting away with it? And what lies in store for those of us who do?

Talking purely as a species now, I reckon we've got to be looking at extinction. Forget about World War III and Atomic Armageddon and alien invasions because we don't need them. We're already doing it to ourselves. I mean you simply can't dilly-dally with all the basics to such an extent without doing yourself and future generations incalculable harm.

Nature simply won't allow you and she's the one in charge. It's all right though, don't panic, us here and now have nothing in particular to worry about. Like with everything in nature, extinction is a painfully slow process (the dinosaurs took about a million years to turn up their claws), but we've certainly got ourselves pointed in the right direction and that's a start.

Yeah, okay this whole argument's been going around for donkey's years so I won't lecture any further. All I wanted to say was that Sally's illness really got me thinking about a few things that actually mattered and for the first time in my life my eyes were open.

Also, cancer's a funny old thing, because it's a disease that comes from within. It's not like AIDS or rabies or Hepatitis or flu where you can point at one bloke/needle/bat and say "he's the one that gave it to me, he's the one to blame" because you've given it to yourself. But that's a hard nut to swallow, so people start looking around for others to blame.

Tobacco companies, drinks companies, petrol companies, battery farmers, dairy farmers, mobile phone companies, pit owners, factory bosses and talcum powder.

It's always everyone else's fault. Never ours.

And there's certainly something to that because it probably is. These industrialists are generally a load of corrupt arseholes who have been poisoning us for the past hundred years or so just to fill their pockets and swimming pools. But that's also wrong because it's not completely their fault. It's yours and mine too because in most case we do have a choice (mobile phone masts and brown sauce being the obvious exceptions). You can choose not to smoke, not to drink, not to live on deep-fat fried micro-chips and not to spend all day downloading ringtones until you've barbecued your fingers.

It's as simple as that. You've got the power.

I'm lecturing again aren't I? Okay, I'll cut it out and end the sermon before I come across as some sort of tree-hugging sissy. There's nothing worse than an ex-smoker/drinker/kebab eater is there?

Anyway, it was everyone's fault and our fault too, but you know what, I really hated being a victim and from what I could tell Sally wasn't too keen on it either, so we made a conscious decision to try and forget about the blame game and concentrate on what we could do to put things right.

People are always saying that you have to stay positive when the chips are down and I really came to believe in these words over the period of Sally's illness. After all, who cares if it was all ICI or Osama bin Laden's fault? Running around moaning and bleating about it wasn't going to do any good, least of all Sally. But a positive, upbeat outlook? You can't put a price on that.

Seriously, sometimes that's the best medicine of all. See, your brain might've got you into this mess, but it also held the power to get you out of it? And I'm not talking about signing over your life savings to Ali Bongo the miracle faith healer or being irritated to death by the eminently punchable *Patch Adams*, I'm just talking about being positive and staying upbeat and believing that you're on the mend, as this can give you the strength you need to get through what you've got to get through.

Which in Sally's case was chemotherapy.

One of the few positives of Sally's chemotherapy was that she could be treated as an out-patient, which was a major plus. Hospitals are grim places at the best of times and just being in them is a constant reminder that you're either sick, pregnant or a doctor. So being able to stay at home was a major plus for Sally.

Her first treatment was scheduled for three o'clock in the afternoon, so we had to set the alarm for twelve hours earlier and get up in the middle of the night so that Sally could take her pre-med. Dexamethasone is how you spell it, but don't ask me how you pronounce it. I still haven't got it right and every time I try to within earshot of a doctor, they almost always turn around and laugh.

The tablets were to be taken twelve and six hours before the start of treatment and sitting next to Sally on the bed as she stared at them in her hand was the beginning for both of us.

"Do you want fresh water?" I asked.

"No," she said, shaking her head. "But I'd love a big glass of wine."

"Alkie," I said. "Oh, and junkie too," I added, when I remembered the pills. Sally smiled and sent the pills down. We went back to bed and lay like spoons until we eventually drifted off to sleep.

It felt like I'd barely got my eyes shut before the alarm went off again, but sure enough it was half past eight. Time to get up and time for Sally to take another dose. Sally rolled her head over on the pillow beside me and shone her pretty green eyes up at me in a way that made me wonder if they'd closed at all last night.

"How are you feeling?" I asked, stupidly.

"Like a million lira," she replied.

"Well, I'm off out with the boys later today. Game of golf, a few pints at lunchtime and curry for dinner. Might even try that new lap-dancing place in Camberley this evening. What are you up to today?"

"Just my chemo," she replied.

"Oh well, don't wait up…" I started to tell her before she stifled my nonsense with a back-breaking embrace.

The worse thing about having an appointment in the middle of the afternoon is that you've got to somehow try to make it through the morning and lunchtime with nothing else on your mind except your three o'clock appointment. I guess this is why they had executions in the morning. Don't get me wrong, I don't think there's ever a good time to fall down a short drop with an even shorter piece of rope tied around your neck, but on the whole, I think if it had to happen I'd rather get it out of the way first thing.

The papers and telly were still packed full of war, death and famine, so I cancelled my subscription with the newsagents and unplugged the aerial to create a sanctuary of positive energy, which sounded like just the ticket – if a bit gay.

However, this did make it somewhat harder to fill in all the silences and distract Sally when she needed distracting, such as this morning, but I did my very utmost and over the past couple of weeks had dug out all our old favourite books, DVDs, craft kits and board games. Unbelievably, that much derided painting-by-numbers kit I got her for Christmas even got the dust blown off its lid.

"When have you got to go back to work? You must've used your entire year's holiday up by now?" she asked. She'd asked me this several times already over the last couple of days but could never remember my answer.

"Oh not for another week. Norman reckons he's having too much fun getting this month's issue out, so he told me to take as much time as I needed."

"Do you think you should go back in a day or so, just so that he doesn't think you're swinging the lead? Or if not, maybe you should just do that report he wanted so that you've at least got something to show for when you go back."

"What report?" I asked, not a clue what she was talking about.

"You know, that report he wanted you to do before Christmas."

I searched the deepest, darkest recesses of my brain and eventually found something that looked and felt about the right shape but I told Sally not to worry about it. "If I've forgotten about it then I'm sure Norman has too."

We spent the rest of the morning and lunchtime filling the hours where we could. Sally took a long, hot bath, washed her hair and plucked her eyebrows, then spent an inconceivable amount of time painting her nails, applying her make-up and getting herself ready so that when she emerged she looked more like she was going to a Royal garden party than a chemotherapy appointment.

"Well, if I've got to feel dreadful, I want to at least look good," she explained, and I couldn't have loved her more had she been holding a gun to a kitten's head and demanding my undying devotion.

Sally's Diary: April 24th

'SIDE EFFECTS' is a funny phrase, isn't it? It makes you think that something small and rather insignificant happens next to the main event. Like a sideshow, or a sidekick, but curiously that's not how side effects feel. The funny thing with my cancer was that it didn't actually hurt. I was tender from time to time and it gave me a little inexplicable indigestion, but by and large we'd always got on quite well. I can't say the same for Taxol. It's been a week since my first session and I'm just about getting over (or used to) the worst of it. My muscles ache and I swing between exhausted and nauseous like a broken barometer. The pins and needles in my fingers sometimes get so bad that I can't hold a pen, and I'm finding it near impossible to hold down some of Andrew's weird and "wonderful" recipes — though I'm not entirely sure how much of that is down to the Taxol. And then, there's my hair. I'm already started to clog up the bathroom plug holes and I know it's only going to get worse, but I can't decide whether to bite the bullet and go for a Sinead O'Connor right away or wait a few more weeks and try to Bobby Charlton it out a bit longer (whose descriptions do you think those are?).

Andrew is currently looking into wigs. He says he read in one of his leaflets that wigs can be important psychological crutches. That maybe so, but they're also pretty expensive. The good ones, that is. Spend anything less than three or four hundred pounds and I might as well walk around with the mop on my head. I know I can get free wigs on the NHS but I think I might dodge the whole wig issue altogether in favour of a hat.

With this in mind, I am leafing through several catalogues in search of a suitable bonnet. I believe they're coming back in fashion. They must be, they seem all the rage in the out-patients' clinic.

CHAPTER 18.
OMINOUS SIGNS

I STAYED IN the car for Sally's first support group meeting. Not because I couldn't bear the thought of having to spend an afternoon surrounded by a load of people with cancer, but because Sally didn't want me to come in with her. She was apprehensive about what lay in store but nevertheless she was determined to brave it alone. She likened it to those sissy first year pupils who cried on the first day of school and who wouldn't let their mothers leave so that every autumn Sally would have to spend a day teaching half a dozen house wives what the letter A looked like. Mind you, she reckoned one or two of them probably needed it.

"Are you sure you don't mind?" she asked when I pulled up into the car park.

"Of course," I reassured her, feeling half-snubbed and half-relieved.

"Okay, I'll see you out here at four. What are you going to do?"

"I don't know. Go to the pub and get slaughtered, I suppose," I replied. Sally said she wished she could come with me, then gave me a kiss and climbed out of the car. "Play nice with the other sickies," I called at her through the wound-down window, then instantly regretted it when one such sicky with no eyebrows and a similar hat to Sally's walked past a split-second later.

They disappeared through the door and into their meeting, so I climbed out from underneath the dashboard and wondered what I should do with myself. I decided not to spend the entire hour staring at the door and set about searching for ways to distract my brain, having not thought to buy a paper and reluctant to go wandering off looking for a newsagents in case Sally needed a quick getaway.

I spent ten minutes playing with the stereo, trying to remember how to store stations on the preset buttons and lost Radio 2 altogether before giving up and looking for something else to occupy my thoughts.

My dashboard was pretty dusty so I found a packet of tissues in the glove box and gave it a wipe, then turned my attention to my wing-mirrors and gave them a spit and polish too until I could virtually see the car behind in them – very unusual for my mirrors. Then I took out all the mats and gave them a bit of a shake. Then I neatly ordered everything in my boot. Then I cleared all the old car park tickets and sweet wrappers out of the compartments down the side of both doors and found a rubbish bin. Then I played with my radio again.

Then I saw how far my seat could recline.

Then I looked at my watch and the door again.

I was just wondering if I should start the car and do a couple of circuits of the car park in order to find a better – nay the best – parking spot when my mobile rang. No number came up to indicate who was calling but I answered it anyway, thankful for the distraction.

"Hello?"

"Andrew, it's Godfrey," a morose voice moaned somewhere off in telephone land.

"Oh, hello Godfrey, where are you?" I asked, checking my watch to see that I only had another fifteen minutes to fill before Sally was finished.

"Well I'm at work ain't I? Where else am I going to be on a Tuesday afternoon?" he pointed out, though his pointing seemed to point more at me than it did in him. See, while Norman had given me a week's compassionate leave to be with Sally when she'd gone in for her surgery, he'd instantly doubled it when the doctors had found more than we'd bargained for and allowed me to throw in my entire year's holiday allocation so that I hadn't actually been anywhere near the office in over six weeks. I was still doing a few bits and bobs on the magazine that either Norman or Godfrey posted or emailed me, including all of my regular columns and features, but the majority of the day-to-day running was being shouldered by Norman, which is remarkable when you think about it. How many other bosses would've done the same? Not many. And even though the workload wasn't exactly breaking rocks for eights hours a day it still spoke volumes about Norman.

"When are you coming back?" Godfrey forced himself to ask, a reticence in his voice a vestige of our recent run-ins.

"Erm… I don't really know. Soon I hope. Another week or two. Why, is everything okay?" Godfrey exhaled deeply into the phone and I had visions of him on the other end of the line screwing up his face and snapping pens in half.

"Fucking Norman…!" he finally grumbled.

"Got you working has he?" I sympathised.

"I don't know what's wrong with him, he can't leave anything alone. Anything," he complained bitterly.

"Why, what's he doing?" I asked, happier than ever to be out of the firing line.

"It's not what he's doing, it's what he's got me doing," he corrected me.

"Okay, what's he got you doing?" I chuckled.

"You know *Caravan Fact File*? He wants to make it twice as big. Twice as fucking big! Does he know how much work that's going to entail? For fuck's sake."

Caravan Fact File was four pages of listings in the back of the magazine which listed all the major manufacturers of caravans, caravan parts and caravan accessories and what they produced. To be perfectly honest, *Caravan Fact File* hadn't changed in almost two years and was in dire need of updating. But they were Godfrey's pages and Godfrey always just used to send the previous issue's off on the first day of the month so that he could cross four pages off the flatplan before the working month had even started. And usually before I'd even finished drawing it up.

"And you know what else he wants? He wants **RRP** prices next to all the listings. And he wants them updated every month. Every single month! I can't do that. How the hell am I going to do all that?" he hyperventilated.

"Well, I guess once you've got the first lot of prices in place it's just a case of faxing or emailing them to the manufacturers each month for any updates and staying on top of it," I reasoned.

"He's even talking about making the whole thing a little A5 pull-out booklet in the centre of the mag, printed on cheap paper, so that people can pull it out and carry it around when they're out and about buying stuff. He doesn't seem to understand that if we do that, we'll then not only have all that extra work to do every month, but we'll then also have to find something to replace *Caravan Fact File* in the back with. He keeps saying that it's an opportunity to try out new features, but it's not, it's a nightmare, it's a fucking nightmare!" Godfrey bawled.

That was probably putting it a bit strong, but try to see it from Godfrey's point of view. Up until Norman had taken an interest in the magazine, Godfrey had been in the enviable position where through routine, forward thinking and the copy and paste keys he'd been able to whittle his regular workload down to about four and a half full days a month – that's spread out across the entire month remember – leaving him free to spend great swathes of his working week surfing the internet, playing on-line computer games, downloading music and movies and disappearing from the office in convenient half hour chunks to have secret pints he thought I didn't know about.

So when you've been used to this sort of cushy existence, extra work and increased responsibilities are always that much harder to come to terms with.

"Please, you've got to come back before he has any more fantastic ideas," Godfrey pleaded.

As much as it amused me to hear about Godfrey's ballooning duties, I wasn't sure I shared Norman's enthusiasm for doubling our workloads. See, new and exciting opportunities are great – in principle, and many's the time I've thought about trying out a new feature, but this can set a dangerous precedent because once you've done it in one issue, you've got to do it in the next. And in the next one after that and the next one after that until suddenly you realise the only way out of this enormous monthly head-ache is to turn your rotten ever-changing pages into a regular monthly feature and before you know it you're copying and pasting *Tow Bar Inventory* every month and crossing off flatplan pages in the pub with Godfrey.

"Look Godfrey, Norman likes to shake things up occasionally, as every publisher does. You never know, it might actually be interesting doing something new for a change, something that's actually a bit taxing rather than just sitting there rotting in your rut and going through the motions," I speculated, though I could've easily added, "all the same, rather you than me mate".

"Oh spare me will you, you sound just like Norman," he objected.

"Well look, it's only for a few weeks, not the rest of your life, so you'll just have to make the best of it. He's not messing with any of my stuff is he?"

"Not for the moment, but you should be warned that he's talking to the repro house about making Tom's mag 148 pages, 120 of them editorial. You might want to tell Tom to hurry up and learn to walk again before he finds himself editing a fucking catalogue."

Jesus, Godfrey was right, this was getting out of hand. I had to get back there.

"Okay, I'll try and get into the office some time before the end of this week and maybe speak to Norman and see if he'll let me take the mag back over on a part-time basis. In the meantime try and look as busy as you can for eight hours a day so that he doesn't saddle us with any more improvements."

"Will do," Godfrey agreed, before catching me by surprise and wishing Sally all the best.

"Thanks," I told him, happy that the worst seemed to be over between us, albeit only in the face of a common enemy.

I now heard muffled murmurs his end and asked the palm of Godfrey's hand if everything was okay before Godfrey came back on the line with a fresh case of grumbles and told me that somebody else wanted to speak to me. I braced myself to hear Norman launch into one about how he'd decided that we should deliver the magazines on BMXs ourselves but it wasn't Norman who tickled a "hello" into my ear.

It was Elenor.

"Oh, hello," I replied, a little unsure about which way this one was going to go.

The last time I'd seen Elenor was in the office some six weeks ago. And an ice-cold blank page of herself she'd been too. She'd talked to me, of course, when she'd needed to, but I suspected that this was only because ignoring me would've been too telling. So, all her counters had been reset to 0000 and we'd spent a few minimalistic weeks of economic interaction, which, when all was said and done, had been something of a blessing as it drew a very thick line under… all that silliness.

All that silliness?

Okay, I'll admit it: all *my* silliness.

For a few weeks I'd walked around with my head up my arse and I still shake my head and wonder how I could've let myself get so carried away. I can't explain it. I really can't. I guess I'd just enjoyed the fantasy while it had lasted, but wasn't quite so keen on it when it almost became a reality.

But I can't do anything about that now. All I can do is learn from my mistakes – or near-mistakes, as my old friend from Frimley Park Hospital would say – move on and spend the rest of my life trying to make it up to Sally. Perhaps without letting on too specifically what I was trying to make up for.

I just hoped Elenor felt the same way.

"We're all missing you Andrew. I'm missing you in particular," she told me just a trifle less huskily than that dog who used to say "sausages" on *That's Life*.

I see.

"Well, yes, thank you. I hope to be back as soon as I can. I just need to be with Sally, my wife, for the moment and do all

I can for her, but I'll pass on your best wishes and I'm sure I'll see you all soon," I told her, without Elenor having given me any wishes to pass on.

Naturally, this gave her the wrong idea entirely.

"Oh, I understand. Is she there with you then?"

"No, not at all. I'm in the car waiting for her to come out of her first support group meeting," I told her, then instantly regretted this and wished I'd lied.

"Oh well, don't worry, no one's listening this end. Godfrey's gone off in a sulk and Norman's back in his office for the moment," she reassured me, then asked if I'd be coming up for Emmeline's leaving do on Friday. "Everyone's going to be there," she promised, prompting visions of me standing around in some God-awful Croydon boozer, laughing and joking with Elenor, Rosemary, Norman, Godfrey, my miserable designer Adam, the *Xtremers* and the sandwich man while my wife made a super-human effort to crawl to the bathroom back home to vomit blood into the toilet.

"Tempting," I told her. "But I don't think so. My wife needs me and…" I took a deep breath, "I think I'm probably going to give work parties a miss from now on, if you know what I mean."

Elenor didn't and told me not to be so boring.

"Actually, I think I'm going to be very boring from now on. Very, very boring," I promised her, to which Elenor pointed out that this was boring. "Yes, I know, but I like boring. And my wife likes boring, so I think I'm going to be the most boring man in the office from now on."

Elenor turned this over in her mind and told me that it didn't bother her one way or the other what I did with my life, it was mine to lead and I could do what I wanted with it.

"I could never be boring though," she told me, rather boringly. "I've just got to go for it."

"Well then you go for it and have fun on Friday. Oh and please pass on my apologies to Emmeline," whoever the fuck she was. At that moment, women in hats started emerging from the building and I looked at my watch. It was just gone four.

"Anyway, I've got to go as Sally's meeting has just finished. Tell Godfrey to give me a call if he has any more problems and I'll see you sometime next week probably. Okay then," I quickly told her, then hung up just as she was in mid-tantalise.

"I'm looking forw…"

Sally emerged from the hall looking a lot happier than she'd done when we'd first arrived. She was in deep conversation with another eyebrowless woman, but took a moment out to wave enthusiastically in my direction.

I waved back and almost choked on the love I felt for her, such was the contrast in feelings I had for her and the girl I'd just spoken to. My God, she was great. Just looking at her chatting and smiling with that other cancer lady. My wife was absolutely fantastic. Absolutely.

And wasn't I a big dummy? Christ!

The smile slipped a little from my face but I tried not to dwell on my own shortcomings and put a positive spin on my conversation with Elenor.

If nothing else, I'd at least proved to myself that her spell was well and truly lifted and that I knew I'd be able to work opposite her from now on and feel nothing but deep disappointment with myself for the way I'd behaved.

No matter how boring that was of me.

Elenor probably wouldn't believe me at first and I could envisage a set of circumstances where she might even try to reinitiate my interests. Not because I was so utterly desirable you understand, but because I wouldn't rise to her flirting from now on. But I was confident I could cope with anything Elenor threw at me. I felt vaccinated. Inoculated against her feminine charms. And it was then that I finally realised that my old friend from the hospital had been one hundred per cent right about everything.

It really was better to be tempted and to pass temptation than to never be tempted at all. At least, I reckon it had been in my case. Because it finally made me realise what I had. And just how lucky I was.

"Hello you," Sally said, climbing into the car and giving me a welcoming kiss.

"Hello you," I replied, returning her kiss. "Let's go home."

Sally's Diary: May 3rd

I MUST SAY, I'm somewhat relieved to have attended my first meeting and lived to tell the tale. I don't know what I was expecting, something like a cross between Alcoholics Anonymous and a sinking lifeboat I suppose, where one-by-one we all stood up and admitted we were dying, but we were not afraid, in exchange for a round of applause and a cup of tea. But it wasn't like that at all. Once I got over my initial jitters, I found I really… well, not exactly enjoyed it, but I took a lot from it. We played the inevitable game of top trumps with our CA125 counts, which I'm glad to say I didn't win, but for the most part we just chatted about our experiences and shared what we'd learnt along the way. Forewarned is forearmed as they say. A lot of the other women were further into their treatments than I so I was happy to sit and listen for most of the meeting, although by the end I'd found my voice.

You know the sad thing that never occurred to me up until this point is that it's not only women with partners who get cancer. Single women get it too. A number of those I talked to this afternoon, Joan in her fifties and Sarah in her mid-forties, are having to go through this whole process alone. Well, not quite alone, as Joan has two children of university age, and Sarah has friends and family close by, but neither has a regular partner to speak of. Sarah was divorced four years ago and hasn't even told her ex-husband about her illness, which I find bonkers, though perhaps it wasn't the most amicable of separations. And Joan is widowed, though I don't know for how long. I didn't like to pry. Either way though, it just goes to show that the expression is right; there really is always someone worse off than yourself.

Which is why I guess these support groups are so important. And not just for single women like Sarah and Joan, but for all of us. Because we're drawing strength from each other. Andrew's been like a rock and I don't think I could've coped without him, but it feels good to be part of something which is helping others too.

I'm looking forward to next week already, though not quite as much as I looked forward to seeing Andrew at the end of my meeting.

It's funny how it sometimes takes misfortune before you realise just how fortunate you are.

CHAPTER 19.
TO LAVISH A GIRL WITH COMPLEMENTS

IT'S FUNNY, but when you're fit and well, most of us are pretty cynical about anything we can't get over the counter at *Boots*. Fall ill or experience some sort of calamity and before you know it we're filling our pockets with charms and drinking the bark of Chinese trees. That's just the nature of life, I guess. We'll pin our colours to any mast that'll give us hope, and that's no bad thing in the long run. There are no atheists in foxholes, as they say.

I started reading up about all this sort of thing on the internet and after a little initial eye rolling I actually found some of it quite interesting. Okay sure, we weren't going to cancel the chemotherapy in favour of having some elderly hippy dangle crystals over us every Wednesday but there was nothing to stop us from opening our minds and broadening our approach to Sally's illness.

The key word to complementary therapies is "complementary", as opposed to alternative.

Now, I'd already sorted out Sally's diet for her so that we were eating the right foods to flush her toxins out and the brand spanking new osmosis water filter was bolted in and providing us with good, clean tap water, so next I looked at what else I could do.

Green tea; this was a revelation. Why hadn't anyone told me about green tea before? According to the book, it could not only help people avoid cancer, it could also help people fight it by limiting the cancer cells' production of urokinase. Startling (whatever they were). Why weren't there billboard posters up and down the country proclaiming this fact? I mean Christ, if they can paper the land with adverts for chicken dippers and cocopops, why can't they do the same for green tea? Admittedly, it tastes pretty disgusting, but then again so do chicken dippers and cocopops, so what's the difference?

"I think it's one of those things you get used to," I reassured Sally, as her eyes pleaded with me for a cup of PG and a HobNob.

"Are you drinking it as well?" she asked.

"No, I thought I'd have an Irish whiskey and a chocolate éclair. Of course I'm drinking it," I replied, and did just that to prove it was safe. "Delicious," I gasped, smacking my lips.

"Really?"

"No, not really. But then things you have to get used to never are, are they?"

And the fun didn't just stop with green tea. We had all sorts of mad and mysterious teas; dandelion & burdock, cinnamon, liquorice, prickly ash and hawthorn and other such treats. I learned about them on the net and read up about the beneficial properties of each, then found a herbalist who lived a short car journey away and got her to mix me up a few batches. She was a nice old stick and served me with such a warm smile that I could've sworn she recognised me from one of her previous lives. She seemed to know what she was banging on about too and tailored the teas to Sally's exact requirements.

"Where do you get your ingredients?" I decided to ask, just as I was leaving.

"ICI. Most of it's just left-over paint scrapings," she replied.

"What?" I gawped, but the lady just smiled:

"Nature."

"Oh. Oh right," I replied, then nodded. Who would've thought: a herbalist with a sense of humour?

Most of the teas were also pretty disgusting but none of them came close to my own attempt at making nettle tea. I'd read up about it on the internet and convinced myself that I could boil anything down I found in a field just as good as Andy McNab or my comedy herbalist friend, so I gave Tom a call and asked him if he wanted to give me a hand.

"What, nettles? Stinging nettles? Are you serious?"

"People have been drinking it for years. It's meant to be very nice," I told him.

"I'll have a fiver on that," he replied.

"Well, perhaps not nice, but you know, good for you."

"Make that a tenner."

Tom was up and out of his wheelchair these days and moving about on sticks. He walked along like a new born giraffe and was just about as stable, a point he proved the following afternoon down the common when he leaned too far forward picking nettles and went face-first into a great big dirty ditch full of them.

God that was funny. I can't ever remember laughing so hard in all my life and Tom just kept setting me off again every time he pointed his tingling, speckled scowl in my direction.

"What happened?" Sally asked, when we got home.

"If I was you I wouldn't worry about me. I'd worry more about what you're having as an aperitif tonight," Tom replied.

Anyway, we boiled it all up, stunk out the house and it was truly disgusting, so we tipped the rest of it away and decided to stick with my humorist's home brews. I mean, they might've been horrible too but at least someone in a white coat had told us they were good for us.

"Are you stopping for dinner Tom?" Sally asked.

"What is it?"

"Mushrooms – shitake mushrooms – fried in garlic with onions, ginger, turmeric and brown rice and with a green salad," I told him.

"Why?" he asked, suspiciously.

"Shitake mushrooms are officially," I underlined, "recognised in Japan as cancer fighting fodder."

Tom weighed it up. "Go on then, I'm game. Besides, if it's horrible, I can always get myself kebab on the way home with that tenner you owe me."

"Huh?"

I tried many of these sorts of recipes and some of them took a bit of getting used to and some of them were actually all right, but the main thing was that they were helping Sally. She'd now undergone her second instalment of chemotherapy and was listless and weak all over again, but the difference this time around was that she was starting to believe – and that was half the battle.

Before, when there'd only been bad news and all the agonies were raw, it had been practically impossible to pick her up off the ground. Sally had seen only doom and gloom and no hope or even reason, but I'd done everything in my power to batter this out of her with a constant bombardment of buoyancy and rosiness that would've seen the average person tunnelling to escape me. Fortunately Sally was far too weak for that sort of nonsense and had to endure all I could throw at her until her spirits finally waved the white flag and started to lift.

Well, you can't stay downhearted forever. Your mind simply won't let you. It's just too much like hard work. Something always has to give and I wasn't going to chuck in the towel until it did.

She even tolerated shower time, which was hot and cold, hot and cold, alternately, to give her lymph circulation a kick start and helped oxygenate her tissues and drain away toxins, though first time around was something of a punch-up.

"Oh my God! Turn it off! Turn it off!"

"Chilly is it? Blimey yeah, that's like ice on my fingers," I said, testing it myself as I splashed it all over Sally.

"Turn it off, Andrew seriously stop it! STOP IT!"

I twisted the hot tap and the water flowed warm again, bring Sally and our next-door neighbours merciful relief.

"You *fucking dickhead*, that was far too cold Andrew. That was bloody freezing."

"You know, you really shouldn't call the bloke in charge of the taps a fucking dickhead. That's not sensible."

"No Andrew don't, I don't like it…"

"Get ready for the cold stuff."

"Andrew, nooooOOOOOHHHHH!"

"That's it love, you scream. Screaming is supposed to be good for you too. Hmm, now where did I read that?"

Of course, in between the fun and games of bath and meal times, Sally was still deeply despondent about the fact that we would never have children but, like with the green tea, the weird mushrooms dinners and the ice cold hosings, it was something she was learning to live with. Still, every now and again I'd catch her feeling the corners of the bedclothes or staring blankly at her toothbrush in a particular way and when this happened, I'd rush in and quickly head off her thoughts with a hug.

Sometimes it worked.

Sometimes it didn't. But this was how we filled our days.

I tried to find as many practical solutions to Sally's

condition as I could and scoured the internet and almost melted the telephone talking to her various support groups, phone friends and all the experts that were generous enough to spare me a few moments of their precious time, although this wasn't all entirely for Sally's benefit.

The plain simple truth of the matter was that I couldn't bear to sit still – figuratively and literally. I just couldn't do it.

Not even for five minutes.

I had done so in those first few days after diagnosis but that was only because back then I didn't know what else I could do, but it had nearly driven me so far out of my mind that I couldn't think to breathe.

And there was another reason I tried to keep busy.

Back at the start, when there were only worries and fingernails and worst fears, my thoughts would occasionally stumble upon questions I didn't even want to ponder. Questions such as:

What if the cancer spread further still?

What if the chemotherapy didn't stop it?

What if Sally were to die?

What would I do then?

I hated thinking these thoughts but once Pandora's lid was lifted there was nothing I could do to stop them from tumbling out. It was awful. And the more I allowed myself to think about these things, the more specific my questions would become.

Bizarre practicalities started taking shape such as how would I pay the mortgage? The amount we'd borrowed had been based on both of our salaries, so did that mean I'd have to sell up and move somewhere smaller? Or would Sally's life insurance provide enough to meet the payments? We were both on a policy and had been since buying our home but it had never meant anything more to me other than an itemised £20 direct debit on my monthly bank statement for sundry whatevers. I'd never expected to actually have to do anything with the policy in practical terms other than renew it once a year and remember to leave the paperwork somewhere obvious for my kids or Battersea Dogs Home to find when I kicked the bucket. Not my problem.

But suddenly it was my problem.

And I didn't know how it worked.

Did I have to fill out a load of forms and supply a death certificate before they'd look at my claim? Or would I have to appoint a lawyer to take care of it all? And what if I didn't want the money? Couldn't I just have Sally back and the insurance company could keep their money along with all the subs we'd ever paid? If I did collect, would everyone think I was a greedy bastard for doing so when my wife had only just passed away? Wouldn't it be better if I gave it all to a charity and not even grubby my hands with it? Would Sally prefer that? Probably not, but would she ever have to know?

And did it come as a cheque or would they just pay it straight into my bank account?

What if they Welshed and didn't pay at all? Could they do that and what if they did? Would I get my lawyer to pursue them through the courts and get what was morally and lawfully mine? Or would I let them keep it and not sully Sally's memory with a legal tug-of-war over a most unwelcome windfall?

I was savvy enough to know that death was a time when people were at their most vulnerable. How many rightful riches had been signed away through tears and turmoil only to be regretted once the mourning had passed? I didn't know but I would've guessed a lot. And it wasn't just insurance companies I had to be wary of either; con men and charlatans circled the obituaries just as vultures circled the savannah. Death was money and, as unappetising as it was to me, the world was full of scumbags who made a living out of dying.

A living out of dying? I thought about that for a moment and wondered if I'd intended it as a pun. I didn't think so but then I started trying to think up other death puns and only stopped when I suddenly remembered what had started me in the first place.

And then I'd feel awash with guilt: guilt for filling my head with such trifles; guilt for missing the bigger picture and guilt for killing off Sally before she'd even begun her therapy.

It was a truly terrible time. What sort of a man was I?

I'd beat myself to bits in an effort to shame any such thoughts out of my head, but they'd never slip very far beneath the surface and before I knew it I'd be at it again, wondering how funeral directors worked and when was the right time to ask Sally if she wanted to be buried or cremated or shot out of a cannon into the sea and how did they sort out the ash of the person out from the ash of the casket and so on and so forth until I was ready to stick my head in the oven in an effort to shut out these terrible thoughts.

I know it sounds callous but really you have no idea how much these questions tortured me. I hated thinking them but I couldn't help it. I guess I've always been a daydreamer and my mind has a habit of wandering and this was just how my fears manifested themselves. It was too vast and too terrifying a scenario to deal with the emotional side of my fears so these trivialities and niggles would fill the void until I was able to distract myself with the dinner or the washing or the shopping or such like. Then sure enough, a few minutes would slip by and I'd feel confused and miserable over splurging so much thought on pots and pans when Sally was sick upstairs and the whole process would start again. A jolt of dread would jog Sally's funeral into my mind and the image would fester until a dozen different tentacles reached into every little corner of my imagination and pulled out a jumble of disjointed worries. I simply couldn't help myself. It was like a sore I couldn't stop picking.

It reminded me of when I was little and I first realised my parents were going to die. There I was, happily tucked up in bed with Winnie the Pooh under one arm and a plastic M16 under the other. I'd had a great dinner of chicken dippers and alphabetti spaghetti and got to stay up late watching Dave Allen, but all of a sudden all I could do was cry. Why? Because for some unknown reason it had suddenly occurred to me that the big, wonderful lady and strong, reliable man downstairs weren't always going to be around for me. In fact, one day both of them were going to die and this wasn't an if or a maybe, this was an absolute definite.

One day mum and dad were going to die.

And there was absolutely nothing I could do about that except worry, panic and cry until I heard the thump-thump-thump of reassuring footsteps on the stairs.

But there were no reassuring footsteps on the stairs for me these days because now I was those reassuring footsteps. And it was my turn to go thump-thump-thumping up the stairs to answer the sounds of crying.

I unburdened as much as I could on Tom, first of all at his place and later at Camberley Leisure Centre while we both trod water (part of Tom's rehabilitation), but for most of the time these thoughts were mine to fret over alone.

So I did what I could to keep them from my mind and

found that the best way was to fill my mind and my days with positive action.

Because unlike my parents, it wasn't right that Sally should die before me. And not just because she was younger, healthier and had Mother Nature's three year bonus that women always got over us men, but because there *were* things that could be done; practical things. And by me. I might not have been a doctor, I might not have been a radiographer and, as my old friend at Frimley Park had correctly pointed out, I certainly wasn't a nurse, but I could still help all the same. He was right about that, just as he'd been right about everything.

And so that's what I did; I helped. Or at least, I tried to. And the more I did, the more I found there was to do. And the more I found there was to do, the more it felt like I was actually helping. And the more it felt like I was helping, the further I was able to pack those awful unthinkable thoughts back into the shadowy corners of my brain.

So I dedicated my days to doing what I could and I made this my routine.

Though more accurately it could better be described as my therapy.

Sally's Diary: May 11th

I'M NOW completely bald and pastier than I've ever been in my life. I look like a deflated Michelin Man and feel like one too. When the doctors warned me about hair loss, I thought they were just talking about my head, I didn't realise they meant all of my hair. But that's exactly what's been disappearing down the plug each this week, and a pink and peculiar version of myself it's left behind. Still, as Andrew is constantly trying to drum into me, you have to put a positive spin on everything, so here goes:

Take two bottles into the shower? Not me, I just use a chamois leather. And how wonderful it is not to have to shave my legs or armpits anymore. What a chore that had become! My legs are now naturally silky smooth, if a little knobbly around the knees, and my pits are stubble free. As for my eyebrows, I no longer have to pluck, I simply erase and redraw until they reflect my mood, although I need to get a lot speedier with the pencil if I'm going to convince people with my look of surprise.

And my bikini line? Well, I guess Andrew finally gets one of his kinkier wishes after all.

CHAPTER 20.
DON'T ASK THE FAMILY

ONE OF THE trickier aspects of Sally's illness was what to do about her parents. Sally had been reluctant to say anything before her surgery because she'd been hoping to waylay the inevitable "all hands to the panic pumps" with reassurances that everything was fine and that the cancer had been dealt with and that it had only been a minor scare and that there was no harm done and lots of good news etc etc etc – but unfortunately, as things turned out, everything wasn't fine, and the cancer hadn't been dealt with, and it hadn't turned out to be a minor scare, and there was considerable harm done, and the resultant news was anything but good.

Which threw up a difficult dilemma.

How did we break it to Ken and Beverley that their little girl was undergoing treatment for a life-threatening illness without the pair of them running all the way over here to set up base camp in our spare bedroom?

It was a delicate one. And a situation both Sally and I were desperate to avoid.

I mean, she was ill and stressed enough without having to cope with her parents as well. I don't mean that in a horrible way but the fact of the matter was it was true. Parents bring stress.

See, left to Ken and Beverley, Sally would immediately have her adult status revoked and be demoted to fragile little princess again, to be bossed, bullied and mothered beyond sanity and told to drink her cancer medicine and eat her greens "like a good little girl and no arguments young missy, you do as you're told".

It was the nightmare scenario. But what could we do? Sally couldn't very well go on telling her parents she was fine indefinitely because sooner or later they were likely to want to come over and see us (or rather her). In fact, a Nicholas invasion was long overdue and Sally was now bald as a tin hat and as pale as parchment. That dreaded phone call had to be made and once it was, how would we ever get rid of them again?

"Righto, well thanks for coming over but Sally's a bit tired now so perhaps it's best if you both said cheerio."

"Say Cheerio? Oh no no no, we're staying. We're not going anywhere while our little girl needs us," they would reply.

"Mum, I'm not a little…"

"Quiet now Sally, you just relax and let Mummy take care of you."

"Mum please…"

"Sally, do as your mother tells you, she knows best, you know?"

"No, just listen…"

"Sally, that's quite enough. And as for you Andrew, you can go. We'll take it from here."

"Hey?"

"She was fine while she was with us, but a few years of being married to you and you've gone and given her cancer. So you can just bloody well go and… er, Andrew?"

"Yes Ken?"

"Where did you get that shotgun from?"

"Superb shooting darling. What now?"

"We could get some more shells and give Norman a quick ring if you liked."

BANG BANG!

"Hmm?"

BANG BANG!

"Andrew, are you going to get that?"

"What?"

"There's somebody at the door."

BANG BANG!

"Oh, oh yeah, sorry, miles away. Just going love."

I hung the last pair of Sally's pants on the radiator and put the washing basket away under the stairs before heading up the hall to see who was laying siege to our front door.

BANG BANG BANG!

"Yes all right, hold your horses, I'm just coming," I called out, although this just encouraged the banging even more and when I opened the door I found an ashen-faced Ken and a frantic Beverley staring at me in white-eyed horror holding their suitcases.

"My God, where is she?" Beverley screamed.

I barely had time to get my thumb pointing in the direction of the stairs before she was steamrollering passed me and sprinting for the bedroom.

"We came as soon as we could," Ken told me.

"You're not kidding are you?" I replied, checking my watch and doing a few mental calculations.

"We couldn't stay away," he informed me.

"Did you even try?"

"Upstairs is she?"

"Yes, I've been locking her in the attic because she looks so horrendous."

"That's not nice Andrew. I hope you don't let Sally hear you saying things like that."

"No, I promise, around Sally I just wring my hands with despair and wail about how terrible it all is and save the jokes for the boys down the pub."

"Are you even taking this seriously? Our little girl's got cancer and she needs…"

That was it. And in record quick time too. Something snapped inside me and I went all the way with it.

"What Ken, what? What does she need? Go on, do tell me what because this is obviously something I haven't given any thought to. So go on, come round to my house and stand in my hallway and tell me what my wife needs. Go on, I dare you because I'd love to hear it."

Ken stared at me with uncertainty in his eyes. Being a boardroom big wig I doubted anyone had spoken to him like this for a good few years. I certainly hadn't so he was momentarily lost for words. But he soon found them again and sure enough told me I'd better watch my step.

"Now, you listen here… Andrew, I couldn't give a monkey's about you or anything you have to say. All I care about is that little girl up there and if you…"

Forget snapped, I exploded.

"Right, I've had enough of this already," I said, grabbing Ken by the scruff of the neck and pointing him in the direction of the road. "Out you go."

"What are you doing? What are you doing?" he countered, trying to prise my hand away from his collar only to trip over his own legs. I managed to sustain his tumble until we were through my garden gate and next to his car, then I dumped him over the bonnet.

"What the hell…"

"In the car or in the house, it's your decision? In the car, you're the fellow in charge, but in the house, I'm the fellow in charge and what I say goes. And that applies to both you and Beverley."

"You can't…"

"Yes I can and yes I am. Now I don't give a monkey's about you either. In fact, you are quite possibly the biggest wanker I've ever met in my entire life. But I do love your daughter and right now yours and Beverley's bullshit is the last thing she needs. And I won't tolerate either of you annoying or upsetting her, do you hear me Ken? So here it is, you're either here to help or you're gone. Both of you."

"Of course we're here to bloody help…"

"Then repeat after me; 'I know nothing'."

"What are you talking about?"

I wagged my finger in his face and shook my head. "No Ken; 'I know nothing'."

"I'm not putting up with this nonsense."

"Ken, I'm going to give you five chances to get it, then you and Beverley are gone; now say it; 'I know nothing'." Ken told me not speak to him that way then tried to barge past me again but I stepped in his way to block his path.

"'I know nothing'," I demanded, refusing to budge.

"Get out of the way," he shouted.

"I know nothing!"

"I'll knock you into next week you little bastard, then you'll know nothing at all!" Ken shouted, blood corpuscles popping all over his face as he tried to shove me aside. But I had a strength I couldn't believe coursing through my veins and I managed to hold him back from the gate. "Get out of my way!"

"I… *know… nothing.*"

"Get…"

You know what, there's just no talking to some people. All Ken wanted and all Ken could see was getting past me and inflicting himself on Sally, but I couldn't, wouldn't and wasn't about to let that happen, especially in his indignant self-righteous extremes and in the ensuing scuffle I ended up 'accidentally' punching him in the gob.

That's right – me. Unbelievable. I punched my father-in-law in the gob.

I lived the dream.

Ken went down onto one knee and I debated for about half a second whether or not to finish the job with the watering can nearby, but I reasoned that probably wouldn't help Sally, so I saved it for another day and gave him a shove to put him on his back.

Ken tried to get back up but I stopped his progress with a foot. "Get off of me. Get off of me!" he coughed angrily, lashing out and trying to drag me down on top of him, but I managed to cling onto the car to keep myself from joining him on the pavement. What the neighbours must have thought, I have no idea.

"You're just not listening are you Ken? You're just not listening at all. Ken? HELLO! This isn't about you and this isn't about me, this is only about *Sally*."

At this, he stopped struggling and let go of my shins.

"I don't want to do this, I really don't, but I can't let you go in there with your attitude because you will kill her in three weeks. You really will and you just don't seem to understand this, do you, because you won't fucking listen!"

This finally got his attention and Ken blinked a couple of times, swallowed hard, then told me, "okay. Okay, I'm listening".

"I know nothing?" I asked him, double-checking that his surrender really was complete and unconditional.

"I… I know nothing," Ken reluctantly repeated.

I stepped back and offered him my hand, half-expecting him to slap it away and come back at me with all guns blazing but Ken didn't try anything.

He really had finally got it.

"Everything I say and everything I do is purely in the interests of Sally," I told him, hauling him to his feet. "I have poured over books, I have read up on this. I have searched the internet and talked to doctors and people in her support group and her counsellors and experts, so please open your ears and shut your gob. If I pour her a weird cup of tea that smells horrible instead of a nice cup of Earl Grey, that's because it's good for her. If I make her a dinner that looks like something you wouldn't want to step in, that's because that's good for her. And if I make light of her condition in front of her in order to put a smile on her face, then that's because that's good for her too."

"Yes," Ken blanched. "Yes I see that now."

"Not yet you don't Ken, because you're not staying. And neither is Beverley. Both of you are most welcome to stop the night and drop in and see Sally again in another week's time but they will be flying visits and full of cheer. It's taken me too long to build her spirits up to sit back and watch you blunder over them in your size nines."

Ken started to say something but I cut him short with a point of order. "But..."

"I'm not having you upsetting or stressing her out. She can't handle it, she's too weak and I'm not going to take it, so you're going to have a quiet word with Beverley, then you're both going to put on a couple of smiles, hold your tongues and we're going to have a lovely evening together, because if you don't you can both go home right now. Do you understand?"

He rubbed his face and sucked his teeth then looked at me and frowned.

"Yes, I... I understand," he said, almost making me feel bad by coughing, "I'm sorry Andrew. I'm just upset and I sometimes don't think, you know?"

I wanted to say, "Get away," but instead decided to draw a line under this nonsense and be the bigger man for once.

"Ken, what say we forget this ever happened and go up and check on Sally? I think that would really cheer her up."

Ken nodded appreciatively.

"Whatever you say, Andrew" he agreed, waiting for me to lead the way back into the house.

"No hard feelings?" I asked.

"Not a bit of it," Ken insisted manfully, then brightened up enormously and added; "And I have to say, that was one hell of a punch you threw. One hell of a punch indeed. Have you been going to the gym or something?"

And Ken was right, he did have to say that. After all, Ken wasn't the sort of man who could admit to being floored by any old average caravan magazine editor.

Sally's Diary: May 13th

WE TOLD *mum and dad and predictably they came straight over. They must've been in such a hurry that dad somehow stood on his own jacket because he had dusty foot prints all over his lapel, which is most unlike dad. Predictably mum cried her eyes out the moment she saw me and I thought that was going to be that for the whole weekend, but then Andrew must've said something when I went to the loo because the tears dried up and the conversation barely went near my illness again. This is just as well because I really didn't want to have to go into the whole hysterectomy thing and have mum bawling her eyes out over my failure to have kids earlier. Actually, that's not fair, I'm sure she wouldn't have done that, but I'm glad we didn't have to go there anyway.*

We had a nice tea and played Monopoly until bedtime which I won, but only because mum, dad and Andrew all conspired to let me; mum owning half the board but refusing to put up any hotels because she "preferred the view without them" and dad hilariously reading my Community Chest cards and informing me I'd won an astonishing eight beauty contests in a row (each time with tears in his eyes). They're going tomorrow and that makes me a little sad because we had such a lovely time. Isn't it strange how sometimes it takes the worst to bring out the best in people? They tell me they'd like to come back again next week, if that's okay with me (extraordinary) and I'm genuinely looking forward to it.

CHAPTER 21.
TO EL AND BACK

I FINALLY STARTED back at work after God-knows how many weeks off and Norman looked almost sad to see me return. He spent the morning talking me through all the editorial initiatives he'd spearheaded, most of which looked like a staggering amount of extra work, then he announced he was off to do the same to Tom's mag, which was some consolation at least.

Godfrey welcomed me back like a long lost father and Elenor was unnervingly civil, brushing the last few months under the carpet as if they'd never happened. Once again I'd forgotten all about Elenor in the wake of what was happening with Sally but it all came flooding back the moment I saw her again and I suddenly remembered what a tricky customer she could be at times. Still I was beyond caring to be honest, so for the sake of peace and quiet I accepted her civility with good grace and tried to forget all about our party incident all over again.

Rather oddly, I found a big card on my desk that had been signed by almost everyone in the company. It was addressed to both Sally and I and it said, "Our thoughts are with you", which was a tad questionable when you considered that the thought of actually posting it hadn't occurred to any of them. I spent a pleasant half an hour going through all the signatures and comparing them to the internal telephone directory to see who'd signed it and who hadn't and found the role call was all too predictable; Rosemary, the *Xtremers*, that bloke in the post room who'd been insisting for longer than I could remember that I owed him ten pounds ever since Leeds had been relegated, despite the fact that I haven't got the faintest idea what he's going on about, and Norman, though that last omission was only because Norman had already sent us (as in actually posted) his own individual card, along with an enormous bouquet of flowers and a box of green tea.

Of those that had signed it, only three signatures included kisses: Pauline (Norman's secretary, who was old enough to be my mum); Adam (our gay designer, who was young enough to be my gay lover); and Elenor (my editorial assistant, who was once again making eyes at me from across the partition).

"I like your hair like that," she said, referring to the skinhead I'd had done to show my support for Sally following the chemo. I'd originally intended to get it all shaved off but Sally had objected, stating that it was bad enough being bald herself without us having to walk around looking like a pair of Hari Krishnas, so I'd opted for a grade one instead.

"Thanks," I replied, trailing a hand across my scalp.

"It suits you," Elenor complemented.

"Yeah, if I didn't know better I would've said you'd been off somewhere on some secret mission fighting behind enemy lines with the SAS," Godfrey said, making me laugh (and swell manfully) at the idea.

"Quiet Godfrey or you'll blow my cover," I played along, but Elenor wanted to play an altogether different type of game and told me again how attractive my new haircut made me look. I decided to nip her flirting in the bud and invented an enormous mountain of work that needed doing before she left for the evening, which did the trick, before getting on with the chore of sorting out my own intimidating pile of work.

Norman had done a bang-up job keeping the magazine on course, but there were still a number of things that had fallen behind schedule.

The worst of these was the caravan park review.

This was something I had to do every month and something which carried the same sort of fear factor that cross country had done when I was at school. I hated it, it was miserable and there was no way out of it.

Okay right, this was the deal. Once a month I had to get into my car, drive to some caravan park, talk to the sub-human criminal scumbag who managed it, take a few photos and write up a review of the place to fill a double-page spread. Naturally, because we were *Caravan Enthusiast* and not *MacIntyre Investigates* our reviews always had to be complimentary otherwise we would've been biting that hand that fed us, so the whole exercise was doubly distasteful. In the seven years we'd been featuring these park reviews (which were Norman's idea, in case you were wondering) I must've done more than six dozen. Obviously, I'd started with the closest parks to the office but these had all been covered so that every month I had to travel further and further a field.

I set Godfrey a challenge to find us a caravan park this side of The Wash but the closest he could manage was a place just outside Boston, in Lincolnshire.

"Are you sure that's the nearest one? What about that place down in Kent you told me about a couple of months ago?"

"No, he didn't want us to come, probably another one full of illegals. He even threatened me on the phone and said he'd kill us if we went anywhere near his place. Stick that in your fact box."

"Fine, Boston it is then. Don't forget to reserve the digital camera this time," I told him.

"What, you want me to come as well?" he asked in astonishment. I stared back at Godfrey and couldn't believe we were going to have to go through this one again.

The park review was a two-man job. Besides driving up there, map reading and finding it in the first place, there was a lot to do once we were there; interview the manager, interview the guests, compile fact box stats, general overview and snap off fifty or sixty photographs to ensure we had enough usable images to satisfy our ultra-precious designer.

One person could do it all at a push, as indeed I had done on a number of occasions when Godfrey's sulks had become too unbearable to share a car with, but I would be damned if I was going to let him off the hook yet again when I had better things to be doing tomorrow evening myself. A trip to Boston meant I'd be late home as it was. I wasn't about to make myself even later just because Godfrey didn't want to miss *Newsround*.

"Yes Godfrey, I want you to come as well. I'm not doing it all on my own again tomorrow and no arguments, so make sure you're here by nine and wearing a suit."

"This is unbelievable!"

"No Godfrey, this is not unbelievable, this is part of your job description."

"I don't think so, Andrew. You show me where it say in my contract that I have to come in half an hour early to go to Boston."

"Godfrey…"

"I'll tell you what, let's flip for it; heads or tails?"

"No, that doesn't…"

"Fine, I'll call. Heads. [flip] There, see, I don't have to go."

Needless to say, this argument went on all afternoon and

equally needless to say, Godfrey didn't turn up for work the next morning. I waited until ten o'clock in an effort to catch him sneaking in late when he thought I might've already set off but Godfrey didn't show up at all.

I tried his mobile, to no avail, and even thought about digging out his address but Elenor told me that wouldn't do any good.

"He's got a job interview this morning," she told me. "Didn't he tell you?"

"No."

"Probably thought he could get away with it while you were on park review and not have to book it off as holiday," she grassed.

"The little bastard. Why couldn't he have just told me yesterday instead of letting me sit here like a duck egg half the morning making myself even later?" I fumed, looking at my watch and screaming inside.

"Don't know, wanker ain't he?" Elenor speculated then added; "Look, do you want me to come with you? I can use a camera and take notes just as good as that virgin."

As much as I needed the help, I wasn't exactly bowled over by the idea. Did I really want to spend a whole day in a car with Elenor and all the baggage that came with that situation? If you'd asked me a few months ago I would've probably looped-the-loop but now the idea just left me cold.

On the other hand, I did need someone's assistance if I was to get back home before nightfall and one phone call aside Elenor and I had never really gotten the chance to clear the air, so I figured I could kill two birds with one stone, although knowing how mischievous Elenor could be at times I was equally aware that I could be letting myself in for a day from hell.

But then I thought, hang on a minute, what am I talking about? A day from hell was waiting in the hospital as doctors operated on your wife to discover the extent of her cancer. A day from hell was trying to pick her up after she'd been told she would never fulfil her dream of motherhood. A day from hell was every day you had to wait to find out if the chemotherapy was working.

Sitting in a car for a few hours with a flirtatious young colleague I was foolish enough to once lust after didn't even come close.

"Okay Elenor, you're on. Grab some petty cash from accounts and the digital camera and I'll meet you downstairs."

*

The journey to Boston was encouragingly uneventful. We talked about work and the telly and then about Godfrey's mystery job interview, and even a little about Sally, then Elenor announced the thing we needed was music and spent the rest of the journey playing with the radio and flipping from station to station every time a song came on that she didn't like. Which was every other song.

After a brief bite and a cup of tea on the A16, we found the caravan park a little after two o'clock and got to work.

The manager was a guy called Chris who was so full of himself that I wondered how he got into his shoes. He bored me to pieces about his life and expanded every point almost beyond comprehension until I was ready to uppercut all six of his chins.

"… because the thing you have to understand about natural drainage is…"

"Actually Chris, can I stop you there?" I finally interrupted. "That's absolutely tons and tons of information and I've got to get on."

"No, can I just make this last point?"

"Seriously Chris, that's more than I could use over four articles."

"It's an important point young man," he exclaimed, incredulous at being stopped in full flow at such a crucial juncture.

"Nevertheless, I've really got enough," I told him, folding my notepad to illustrate this fact.

Chris wasn't to be deterred and carried on regardless, as if the meat of his point would somehow rekindle my interest and cause me to phone the repro house to "stop the presses". Alas, there wasn't any meat to his point. In fact, he barely had a point. He just wanted to moan about his job and savour the experience of having someone listen to him for a change.

"… because it doesn't do itself, you know…" he was saying, as he hung onto my elbow and followed me outside.

"Yes yes I understand. Thank you. Thanks very much, that's great." I continued to try to repel him until I spotted Elenor halfway down the park taking snaps of a couple of elderly holidaymakers.

I caught her attention with a wave and pointed to my watch to ask her how much more she had to do but Elenor just came bounding over with girlish enthusiasm. I wondered if she'd still be bounding after another seventy of these park reviews.

"I was just talking to those people," she informed me, cutting right across Chris's diatribe as if he wasn't even there. "They've been coming here for sixteen years. They must be mad."

Something had changed and it took me a moment to realise what. Chris had stopped talking. I turned around to double-check he hadn't fallen into one of his drainage sink holes and saw that he'd completely clammed up in the presence of my vibrant young colleague. I took the opportunity to thank him once more in order to draw a line under our acquaintance but Chris just mumbled something about it all being part of the job as he tasted Elenor with his eyes.

"One thing I haven't got is any interiors. The old lady didn't want to invite me in because her caravan was a bit of a mess and I can't seem to find anyone else at home," Elenor explained.

I asked Chris if he had any vacant caravans we could look inside and he sorted us out with a set of keys. "Pitch 38, half way down near the wash hut," he said, barely able to look up in case he accidentally caught Elenor's eye. "I have to get on, just bring them back when you're finished."

"God, what a weirdo!" Elenor remarked, before we were barely out of Chris's office. I wondered if she'd deliberately wanted him to hear or if she'd simply not cared before deciding it amounted to pretty much the same thing. She continued to run Chris down as we made our way over to pitch 38 and let ourselves in to look around.

The caravan was a standard four-berth job with kitchen, main bedroom and fold-down fixtures and fittings and I took the camera from Elenor and took over the snapping, seeing as I knew what needed to be snapped.

I'd just folded back the little bathroom door and was taking a photograph of the chemical toilet when Elenor called me from the bedroom. "Andrew, come in here a moment. Bring the camera."

"Hold on a sec," I replied, filling the bathroom with flashes before pulling closed the door again and making my way through to the bedroom.

When I got there, I could scarcely believe my eyes.

Elenor had stripped down to just her bra and thong and was lying on the bed, trailing her fingers up and down the length of her body.

"Want to take a couple of pictures of me?" she giggled, pulling down one of her cups to flash me a nipple. "Or do you just want to join in right away?"

Some people probably get these sorts of invitations every day; rock stars, film stars, important politicians and casting directors, but for me this was a first and it struck me momentarily dumb. Not because I was considering it, please understand, but simply because my reactions had no precedent to go to and were left fumbling in the dark as to the proper etiquette of such a situation.

Elenor must've taken my hesitation as deliberation because she spooned an extra layer on where it wasn't needed and told me no one would ever know, although I was fairly confident the news would somehow filter its way back to Godfrey.

"Put your clothes on Elenor and stop mucking around," I finally replied, gifting her a get-out to preserve her feelings.

But Elenor didn't want to take it. Much like Chris, she seemed to think if she pressed hard enough she could bring me around and leapt from the bed and stood in front of the door to bar my exit.

"Oh no you don't. I know what you want and I'm not going to let you leave until you've had it," she smouldered. "Now kiss me." She presented me with a pair of pre-puckered lips and closed one of her eyes, but the two-dimensional version of Andrew Nolan didn't fancy her any more than the three-dimensional version had.

"Elenor seriously, we haven't got time for this," I replied, and inserted another get-out for her. "So wind me up when we're back at the office, but let's just get this done and go home, shall we?"

"This is no wind up," she smiled, before attempting to melt around my waist, but I jumped back out of her arms and told her to pack it in.

"No Elenor, no. I don't want to," I insisted, sharpening Elenor's eye and tightening her lips.

"Don't want to! You don't want to!" she steamed. "You wanted to back at the Christmas party though didn't you?"

I thought about lying but figured this would only stir the pot some more so I told her that that was then, this was now.

"You're just changing your mind? Well you can't do that," she spat, taking a big step into my face.

"Elenor. Elenor, please calm down," I implored her, rapidly running out of room in which to retreat.

"Calm down? Calm down? You bastard! Call yourself a man?" she growled, scrambling across the bed after me, while keeping herself between me and the door at all time. "You're not a man, you're just like Godfrey."

"Elenor, this is…"

"I don't care. I don't care at all. What are you going to do? Are you going to run away and cry? 'Boo-hoo-hoo, the little girl frightened me'," she mocked, snapping her bra clasp with one hand so that it fell to the floor. "Or are you going to get me on that bed and show me what sort of a man you really are."

With this, she launched at me, pinned me to the wall and tried to rape a kiss out of me. I did all I could to untangle myself from her but she had more arms than Ganesh and a couple of them almost made it into my trousers.

"NO!" I shouted, pushing her back onto the bed but falling on top of her when she pulled me off my balance.

"I'm married," I told her, but this cut little ice with Elenor.

"You were married back in January and your wife wouldn't have known then and she won't know now, so come on, just fuck me. Fuck me, fuck me! Do it now, I know you want to," she bucked, wrapping her legs around my waist and pounding back against my loins.

I was finally all out of get-outs and squeezed her wrist until she squeaked with pain. Her hold loosened just long enough for me to rip myself from her arms and once I was free I hurled myself through the door and out of the caravan into daylight. I half-expected a witness or two to be waiting for me, but there was no one to note the state of my appearance, so I quickly pulled myself together and straightened my clothes before fat Chris blundered by.

Once respectable, I sucked in a few deep breaths to try and calm my jitters and took stock of what had just happened.

Elenor had lost it. Big time, as it turned out. That was the long and the short of it. Elenor had lost it…

… and it had all been my fault.

I'd started this whole sorry saga and it had ballooned into a nightmare. It didn't matter that I hadn't gone through with it at Christmas or that it took two to tango or whatever other excuse I could think of. All that mattered was that Elenor had believed I was there for the taking because at some point I had led her to believe this. Everything else was immaterial.

What a mess!

Any second now she was going to come through that door kicking and screaming all over again and I didn't know what to do. I'd calm her and I'd talk to her and I'd reason with her but there were going to be consequences from this day's work, of that I was in no doubt.

And this was the last thing Sally needed. All her incredible progress and all her hard work could be undone in one foul and immensely foolish swoop. And next to everything else that was running around in circles inside my panic-stricken brain that was the one thing that really terrified me.

I had to make Elenor understand that this was no longer about me. I had to go back in there and speak to her. I mean, I knew I had to do that anyway. I couldn't exactly just drive off and leave her in the middle of Lincolnshire. No, I had to bite the bullet, grab the bull by the horns, grasp the nettle, seize the day and…

Unfortunately, before I could do any of those things, a blur of hair and colour came bursting out of the caravan and sprinted past me in the direction of the woods. She left me for dead (much as I would've loved to have done for her) and reached the trees before I got my feet moving.

"Elenor, wait!" I called after her, locking my sights onto her red top and tracking her as she weaved her way through the shadows of the trees. But Elenor didn't wait. She just kept on running, through the bracken and around the maze of leaves and branches, desperate to put as much distance between herself and me as she could. "Elenor please," I called again, but Elenor only slowed when she couldn't find a way through the thickening undergrowth and only then to try another route.

At first, I thought she was just running away to inconvenience me. You know, a kind of vindictive ploy to delay our departure and make me even later home, but then I heard a sound that stopped me in my tracks – it was the sound of Elenor crying. I faltered for one indecisive moment then redoubled my efforts to catch up with her.

"Elenor wait, Elenor!" I shouted, charging through the

brush and pleading with her to stop.

"Go away," she cried back weakly.

"Please Elenor, wait."

A branch whipped me in the face and I slipped on ditches, tripped over roots and ran until my shoes were full of thorns, but still Elenor wouldn't stop. She'd had the foresight to wear trainers, so she was better equipped for the terrain, but Elenor was running blind, which gave me the tactical edge. This paid off when Elenor suddenly came across a rusty old barbed wire fence. She turned and followed it along as far as she could go, but then an enormous prickly shrub barred further progress so that I had her cornered. That was when she decided to go through the fence.

I guess Elenor must've had about as much practice of going through barbed wire fences as I'd had of fending off rampant nymphomaniacs because she snared herself halfway through and her sobs quickly turned into yelps as the spurs dug into her skin.

"Ow-uh-uh-uh," I heard her hollering as I caught up.

She'd all but given up trying to yank herself free by the time I reached her and was now crying with pain as she gored herself on rusty wire.

"Help me," she wept, her voice quaking with misery.

"Hold still, Elenor. Just hold still, I'm going to get you out," I told her. I took a moment to quickly assess where she was stuck, then put my foot on the middle strand and pulled on the top strand.

"Ow! Ow! Ow!" Elenor blubbed as she rubbed against the barbs.

Her top was still caught so that when she tried to back out, she pulled herself into the spikes all over again. I told her to keep still and picked her top free until she could safely extract herself, but then her hair and her skirt got caught and it took a little bit more picking until Elenor was finally free.

She stumbled back the moment she was able to and I thought she was going to run off all over again, but instead she just stood there shuddering and nursing her cuts, the picture of human misery.

"Elenor, I'm so so sorry," I said, reluctant to approach her in case I freaked her into bolting again. "Really I am, please, let's just talk a moment."

I found some napkins in my pocket and offered them to her and she took them and blew her nose and dabbed her cuts.

"This is all my fault," I told her. "And I should never have let it come to this, but…" I swallowed hard, "back around Christmas I really thought I wanted you. And I allowed myself to get carried away with the idea. So much so that for one insane moment I forgot I was married."

I edged a little closer and Elenor held her ground.

"But that would've been wrong. So so very wrong, because I love my wife very much and that would've destroyed everything. Please, I hope you see. I was such an idiot. Such a dickhead."

Elenor sniffed.

"I just feel really silly," she warbled, her shoulders now barely six inches apart.

"Don't. God don't. You have nothing to feel silly about," I reassured her, closing to within a couple of feet if her now. "If anyone should feel silly, it's me."

"I'm embarrassed," she sniffed, her mouth a perfect down-turned crescent.

"Embarrassed? What about? I'm the one who's embarrassed," I insisted. "I'm the one who chickened out and ran away if you remember. If anyone should be embarrassed, it should be me. What a wally I am! How boring!"

I placed my hands on Elenor's arms and she instantly fell into my chest. I slipped my arms around her gently and tried not to fling her back into the barbed wire when I felt a load of snot trickle down the back of my neck.

"There there, let it all out," I whispered.

"I'm so unhappy," she suddenly blubbed. "Nobody likes me."

"What are you talking about? Everybody likes you!" I exclaimed.

"No they don't. Nobody does; no one at work, my friends, my mum and my dad? They all hate me," she shook, gasping and wobbling into my ear.

"Oh Elenor, Elenor, Elenor," I sympathised, squeezing her tightly and carefully stroking her back. "Now that really is silly. You're without doubt the nicest, prettiest and loveliest girl I've ever met in my life," I lied, spreading it on perhaps thicker than she deserved, but this wasn't really the time for cold hard truths. "I can't imagine anyone I'd rather have as my editorial assistant. And if I wasn't married and ten years younger, I'd be chasing you all around these woods until you were mine."

I have to admit, this came out sounding slightly rapier than it was meant to, but Elenor didn't seem to mind and continued to sob all over my collar.

It occurred to me at that moment that Elenor and I lived our lives on very different frequencies. Elenor's life sounded as if it were full of ups and downs, highs and lows, adulation and misery, pandemonium and loneliness, whereas mine – up until recently – had been pretty plodding by comparison; calm and steady, cosy and domestic, easy and peasy, comfortable and uncomplicated.

Which of us had the better life?

I guess that's a subjective question. The grass is always greener on the other side and that whole quandary. I didn't know and I couldn't tell you. Not least of all because I was pretty sure Elenor enjoyed some fantastic and memorable highs when the music was pumping, the Cava flowing and me and Sally were in our pyjamas and three hours into bedtime. Yep, I don't think there was any doubt about that. All I really knew was that I wouldn't have traded my lot for hers for all the green tea in China because I was spectacularly happy with my plodding calm, steady, cosy, domestic, easy peasy, comfortable and uncomplicated life. It had just taken an utter calamity for me to realise it.

Now, all I wanted was to have it back. If only I could.

I pulled Elenor from my neck and looked into her puffy red eyes.

"Elenor, you have no idea how lucky you are, do you? You're such a lucky girl," I informed her. "You've got it all; looks, personality, sex appeal and youth. You've got the world at your feet and you don't even realise it. Don't go getting yourself worked up about things you'll be laughing about in a few weeks time. Honestly, life's too short," I told her, running out all the old tried and tested lines in the absence of any wisdom of my own.

"I just want people to like me," she muttered apologetically.

"And they will. I do. But the main thing is you should like yourself first. I reckon that's the secret to life. Find that and everything else will fall into place," I reasoned.

"And if it doesn't?" Elenor asked, not unreasonably.

I thought about this for a moment because she was quite

right, there was a definite flaw in my argument.

"Well," I pondered, "you'll have the most important piece of the jigsaw in place so what does anything else matter?" For a moment, I though Elenor was going to ask what sort of answer was that, but instead she just wrapped her arms around me and gave me a grateful hug.

"Thank you, Andrew," she simpered.

"It's okay. It's okay," I said, then turned my thoughts to her injuries. "I think maybe while we're at it, we should probably get you to a doctor's and get your cuts cleaned up properly. Just to be on the safe side."

Elenor was about to say something in reply when a voice came at us from behind and told us both to pack it in. We looked around and located an elderly lady decked out in tweed who was walking her dog on a nearby path.

"I say, you there, these are public woods. They have children playing in them, so stop that immediately, it's indecent," she was yelling. "Why don't you go home to do that sort of thing?"

This was so ridiculous that I couldn't help but laugh. Elenor soon joined in and the tweed lady strode off purposefully, either to report us or to go home and do her own indecent thing.

"Do you want to get out of here then?" I asked Elenor.

"Yes, let's go," she agreed, then stole a quick kiss before I could do anything about it.

"Just for keepsakes," she told me and smiled.

Sally's Diary: July 26th

I DON'T KNOW how to feel about my last session of Taxol. I'd been counting down the weeks, but now that it's come I can't help but feel anxious. I'd developed something of a love/hate relationship with my drip. I hated it because it sapped me of strength and knocked me for six, but I loved, or at least, had come to depend on it because it was my treatment. And my treatment was what was helping me fight my illness and lower my CA 125 count. I'd always feared the day when my illness spread out of control and the doctors said, "I'm very sorry Mrs Nolan, but there's nothing else we can do for you. Next patient please", and that's how this feels.

I know it's stupid and that all my test results have come back to show that my cancer is in remission, but I'm still nervous about being cut loose. Of course, I'll have regular check-ups but my check-ups won't be every three weeks, so the trick is learning to believe that my cancer has gone for good and isn't just waiting around the corner for the doctors to turn their backs.

Andrew thinks returning to work will help me slip into my old routine again and Carol agrees. She says the children keep asking after me and this in itself gives me a lift every time I hear it.

I have the rest of the summer to prepare so I can put off any final decision for a little while longer but I'm pretty sure I'll go with Carol's advice. She's an exceptional lady and has always been an inspiration to me.

Perhaps now it's my turn to be an inspiration to others.

CHAPTER 22.
BACK TO SCHOOL

I DROVE SALLY to school her first day back. She could've walked but I wanted to be with her when she picked up her life again. Her last session of Chemotherapy had been back in July and now here in September, with the leaves turning brown and the streets full of children in school uniforms, the world had a comfortable ring of familiarity to it once more.

Tom had come too, which meant we were both going to be late for work this morning, but Norman had given us his blessing and sent his own good luck message to Sally.

"What is it with you and Norman these days? Anyone would've thought he'd adopted you or something?" Sally asked, unclipping her seat belt as we pulled up outside the school gates. I'd always had a bit of a blind spot for Norman in the past, I'll admit, although this was probably just because he represented my job and my little station in life. But Norman had acquitted himself magnificently over these last few months and I couldn't have asked for a more understanding boss or a better friend. Of course there was a reason for all of this, as I'd consequently discovered, and it was the same reason his wife's picture hadn't changed in twelve years. Her fight had been with breast cancer and sadly it had been a fight she'd started too late. But this was something I would keep to myself. No good could come of sharing Norman's motivations with Sally. Better she thought they were driven by pure benevolence than fear. Still, Norman had been Sally's strongest champion and I owed him a debt I could never repay, but which I'd spend the rest of my company days trying (although this didn't actually stretch to my doing his report, as Tom pointed out).

Carol was waiting for us at the gates when we arrived. She came strolling over as we climbed out of the car and gave Sally a welcome back hug she'd clearly been saving up all summer long.

"You're here; the children will be thrilled," she said.

"What, at being back at school? Are you sure?" Tom replied, making Sally laugh and Carol purse her lips in a prickly matronly way. This was Carol's domain and woe-betide any man for suggesting the kids might not actually want to be here as much as she did.

I interjected, telling Sally how lovely she looked to prompt Carol and Tom to do the same before they went for each other's throats and they duly bit with a dozen compliments of their own until Sally was well and truly swamped. Still, it wasn't just to defuse the moment, I truly meant it. Sally did look amazing right now. She'd always been beautiful but in the depths of her treatment she'd been but a paper-thin version of herself. Now with the Chemo ended her glow had returned. The colour had come back to her skin, her eyes again sparkled and her hair had grown almost an inch, enough for her to discard her summer bonnet. She could even fit into her old jeans again, the ones she kept around for motivational purposes, all without having to fork out for [and then cancel] another year's gym subscription. All told she could've almost passed for one of those skinny, cropped Parisian catwalk models – if it hadn't been for the bag of books on her shoulder.

"You run along love and I'll see you tonight," I said, giving her a kiss that belonged more behind the bike sheds than outside the school gates. "Have a great day."

"They all are," she said, giving Tom and I a little smile as she headed on into the playground with Carol to ring the bell. We hung around to watch her go inside before climbing back into the car. Well I climbed in, Tom grunted and groaned. After a summer of arduous physiotherapy Tom now walked like John Wayne in tight trousers with a choc-ice melting in each pocket. It would take a few more months before he was totally grunt-free but there was no rush. The Camberley 5K Fun Run was still some months away and there were plenty of places – which was possibly why Tom still hadn't got around to filling in that entry form I'd picked him up.

"She'll be fine, she's a trooper," Tom assured me unnecessarily and I didn't doubt it. Sally had resources of strength I could only dream of. Only a few months earlier she'd been told she would never have children and yet here she was returning to a job where she'd be surrounded by them all day long and the school board couldn't keep her away. They gave her the choice of postponing her return until after Christmas but they would've had more chance of convincing Godfrey to turn down his new job on a porno mag to stay with me on *Caravan Enthusiast* than they would've at keeping Sally at bay. She'd been a force of nature this morning and I couldn't wait to get home this evening to hear about her day.

"Are you popping over later?" I asked Tom, but he said he couldn't. Kate was coming over this evening and he was taking the phone off the hook. In days gone by he might've given me a suggestive little wink but it wasn't like that with Kate. She was different. She was special. She – he'd even gone so far as admitting to me – was 'the one'.

Well Kate may have been the one for Tom, but she'd been just one of two hundred to Martin who drank in the Duke of

York. He'd pulled her, shagged her and dumped her all within the space of a forgotten weekend, but that weekend hadn't been forgotten by Kate and when she'd finally bumped into him again, out shopping with his wife, life caught up with Martin with a horrible vengeance.

"I guess his wife did mind after all," I said, starting the car to take us both to work.

"Well fuck me, wouldn't you?" Tom replied, and I tried to make out if he'd intended that to come out as some little dig about Elenor, because that's how it had felt, but I let him have it in any case, only too aware of my own passing lunacy.

Still, Tom had bagged Kate on the rebound and things had gone from there. She'd given him a confidence he no longer needed to display and he in turn had restored her faith in men. Really, him? It's funny isn't it how sometimes we need to be broken before we can be fixed.

"And how is Elenor?" Tom then asked out of the side of his mouth.

"See, I knew that was a dig," I said, turning onto the A30 to take us down to the motorway.

"No dig, just a question. How has she been around you?" which in itself could've been a dig.

"She's been fine actually," I told him. "It's helped that Godfrey's left so there's no one to pull the wings off any more, but by and large she's been okay," and she had. We'd talked things through on our way back from Lincolnshire and reset the thermostat to a temperature we both felt comfortable with. Elenor was mortified to have exposed so much of herself to me, both physically and emotionally, but she'd learned something about her own needs and limitations in the process so I guess it had been a worthwhile experience for her. It had certainly been for me so we made a pact that we would never talk about it again, not to anyone (not even Tom), and this oath of secrecy had helped cement a new found friendship.

And did I ever regret not taking Elenor up on her offer?

No, of course not, because I would never have been able to look either myself or Sally in the eye if I had've done. But that's not to say I no longer found her attractive. Her body had been all I'd imagined it to be and every now and again, on occasional slow work days, the memory of Elenor in her underwear would tip-toe into my cubicle to give me a glimpse of what I'd passed up before sauntering away again to rejoin Abigail and in the furthest recesses of my mind.

Well I am only flesh and blood and Nicorette patches you know. To have claimed otherwise would've been a lie. But I was no longer tempted by her. No longer gutted. No longer wondering what I'd missed out on because I now knew I'd not missed out on anything. I'd found a soul mate in Sally, the woman I'd spend the rest of my life with and we'd share the wine and roses and bumps and bruises together come what may. I was finally content that I was exactly where I wanted to be.

But it's funny, if things had worked out differently it could've so easily been Tom instead of me and curiosity once more got the better of me.

"So go on then, in the spirit of honesty, tell me, what did happen between you and Sally back at University?"

Tom looked over and raised an eyebrow. He'd rebuffed me before and I expected him to do the same again but instead he just shook his head and smiled.

"You really want to know?" he asked.

"Nothing you tell me's going to change the way I feel about her," I replied. Tom shifted awkwardly in the passenger seat before finally shrugging and shaking his head.

"Okay. I told her I loved her," he said, and this was so unexpected I thought it had to be a lie.

"Come on don't muck about. Seriously, what did you do?" I urged, figuring he must've tried to stick something up her arse at the very least but Tom was steadfast.

"That's all I did, after just one night together I told her I loved her," he almost laughed. "What a plank!"

If I'd been asked to take a stab at the least likely explanation as to what had gone on between them it would've probably been this. Tom wearing her knickers or Sally fleeing after being led through to a waiting glass coffee table I could've almost seen, but this? It boggled the mind and threw up all manner of questions, the most obvious of which was clearly: "And so do you?"

But Tom just shook his head again. "No of course not. Well, obviously I love her to bits but not the way you mean. Sally's just a friend, nothing more," and I half-expected him to say, "you know, like you and Elenor are?" but he declined the chance. I guess he was too wrapped up lamenting his own foolishness to turn the screw into mine.

"But you did at the time?" I pressed.

Tom just stuck out his lip. "No, not even then. Not really."

"So why did you tell her you did?" I asked.

"Because I was 19. And because she was the first girl I'd gone to bed with. If I'd banged you that night I might've said it to you too," Tom shrugged and I could see his point. We all said and did things we didn't mean when the wine and hormones were flowing and at that age who knew love from the real thing? Not me, that was for sure, and some might uncharitably argue I still had problems in that area so who was I to point the finger? "Besides," Tom continued, "I did you a favour in the end, mate."

"How do you figure that?"

"Well – and don't tell Sally I told you this – I reckon she only went out with me to make you jealous," he said, finally proving the world was more topsy-turvy than I could've ever possibly imagined.

We joined the motorway and headed into town. Somewhere up this road desktops and documents, caravans and colleagues were waiting for us but they'd only prove a temporary distraction.

At the end of the day, I'd come home along this same road again.

Back to Sally.

And to the life we shared.

"There is no duty we so much underrate as the duty of being happy."
– Robert Louis Stephenson, 1881

ABOUT THE AUTHOR

Danny King was born in Slough in 1969 and later grew up in Yateley, Hampshire. He has worked as a hod carrier, a shelf-stacker, a painter & decorator, a postman and a magazine journalist (based for a time in sunny Croydon, would you believe?). He today lives in Chichester with wife, Jeannie, and four children and writes books and screenplays.

Follow him on Facebook at 'Danny King books'.

ACKNOWLEDGEMENTS

My thanks to Jeannie King, John Williams, Clive & Jo Andrews, Katie Finnigan and Simon Fellows and for each helping me with this book. Also to the eagle-eyed Jon Evans for spotting a few wanton typos in an earlier edition. Many thanks to you all.

BY THE SAME AUTHOR

BOOKS
The Burglar Diaries
The Bank Robber Diaries
The Hitman Diaries
The Pornographer Diaries
Milo's Marauders
Milo's Run
School for Scumbags
Blue Collar
More Burglar Diaries
The Henchmen's Book Club
The Monster Man of Horror House
Infidelity for Beginners
The Executioners
The No.1 Zombie Detective Agency
Eat Locals
Dating By Numbers (by Kim_89)
Return of the Monster Man of Horror House

TELEVISION & FILM
Thieves Like Us (2007)
Wild Bill (2012)
Eat Locals (2017)
The Hitman Diaries (2010) – short
Run Run As Fast As You Can (2017) – short
Little Monsters (2018) – short
Seven Sharp (2017) – short
Romantic (2019) – short (Russia)

STAGE
The Pornographer Diaries: the play
Killera Dienasgramata (Latvia)

If you enjoyed this book please consider posting a review or telling a friend as it really really helps. Seriously. Thanks.

Printed in Great Britain
by Amazon